A WALK ON THE CLIFFS

A WALK ON THE CLIFFS

Margo Reasner

iUniverse, Inc.

New York Lincoln Shanghai

A Walk on the Cliffs

Copyright © 2005 by Margo Reasner

iUniverse books may be ordered through booksellers or by contacting:

iUniverse
2021 Pine Lake Road, Suite 100
Lincoln, NE 68512
www.iuniverse.com
1-800-Authors (1-800-288-4677)

This is a work of fiction. All of the names, characters, events, and places are either the product of the author's imagination or are used fictitiously. Any resemblance to actual persons, living or dead, events, or locales is entirely coincidental.

Back cover photograph taken by Nicole LeBlanc, Studio 23, Marlborough MA.

ISBN-13: 978-0-595-36047-5 (pbk)
ISBN-13: 978-0-595-80497-9 (ebk)
ISBN-10: 0-595-36047-5 (pbk)
ISBN-10: 0-595-80497-7 (ebk)

Printed in the United States of America

This book is dedicated to my mother who always told me I could achieve anything I desired; to my husband who kept asking me when I was going to start that book I always talked about; and to my cat, Becca, who kept me company while I was writing.

CHAPTER 1

▼

I never could decide what to pack. I was about to leave to spend a week on the Northern California coast and I had an image of myself looking casually seductive. I wanted everyone to believe that I just threw something on without thinking; a person they would feel comfortable to be around, but also like I was someone they would want to touch. I remembered a cream colored, thick-cabled fisherman's sweater that I had bought with just such an occasion in mind. It, with a pair of denim jeans and some boots, might create the atmosphere I was going for. Then I wondered what Robert would think if I wore this outfit, but reminded myself to return to the task at hand. I spent way too much time worrying about what Robert might think of this or that. My time was now better spent figuring out which clothes to pack so that I wouldn't freeze to death on vacation once the fog rolled in.

Finding warm clothes wasn't going to be a problem in my closet. I live in New England; Central Massachusetts to be exact, in a place where the winters can be frigid and brutal. But what I needed now was a good mixture of casual and nice clothes for both warm and cold weather. And, of course, they all needed to fit into the one large suitcase that lay open on the bed in front of me. Finally, I located the fisherman's sweater in my drawer of winter clothes. I held it up to my body and looked at the mirror, trying to imagine how Robert would see me. I saw a fairly attractive woman in her late twenties with light brown hair, slightly longer than shoulder length, and with the sweater approximating how it would look being worn, I felt that my natural 'girl next door' look was enhanced. Satisfied, I folded the sweater and was able to squish it into the last small corner of available space. As I was latching the lock on the luggage I heard a sound coming from the kitchen.

"Mary Ann… you home?" Brad asked, as he dropped his keys on the table.

"Yes, I'm in the bedroom packing," I said.

"Are you about done yet? We need to get going to the airport if we're going to make our flight," he said.

"Yes, I just finished. Are you sure that you packed everything that you need before you left this morning?" I asked.

"Yes… I've got enough to get by and if we need anything else we can just buy it there. It's not like we're going to a foreign country."

He then came into the bedroom, grabbed both of our suitcases and headed outside to the car. It was at times like this that I was reminded how nice it was to have someone take care of me. Brad was always dependable, as well as fairly predictable after all these years. I quickly looked around the apartment to make sure that all the appliances were unplugged and that the windows and doors were locked. I smiled as I thought about what a comfortable home we had created in seven years of marriage. Everything seemed in order so I closed and locked the door and then hurried out to the car.

The trip to Logan Airport, checking-in our luggage and going through security went uneventfully. After we settled into our first-class seats, we ordered a couple glasses of wine. It was a long trip from one coast to the other and we wanted to be comfortable.

The stewardess brought miniature wine bottles over to us and said, "Mr. and Mrs. Radcliffe, the captain has informed me that we will be taking off on time this morning."

When I heard Brad say "Thank you," in an oh-so-serious tone of voice I started to quietly chuckle to myself.

Brad leaned over to me and whispered, "Hey, stop laughing or they'll know that we've never flown first class before."

I just smiled at him and gently laid my hand over his on the seat rest between us. He had a tendency to be serious and worried about what people thought of him. But it was just that trait that had served him well during our years together. After college he had started a software consulting business with a classmate of his, and a year or so ago he had bought that partner out. The business, which had been doing well with both of them at the helm, blossomed under his lone leadership. At the time of the buy out I had given up my old job and taken on the position of Marketing Coordinator for his company. Although we could easily afford the extra cost of these first-class tickets, it was important to him that people believed that he was born enjoying such luxuries. And it was this same thinking that had kept us from buying our first home. Brad wanted to stay in our small apartment, saving money, until we could afford to buy the only house we'd ever want to own. The idea of a first-time fixer-upper, that we could eventually sell and move up from, never even entered his mind as a possibility. And maybe his way of thinking was correct, because I could see that soon we would be able to afford the home of our dreams.

"Did you get a hold of Robert or Melissa?" he asked.

"Yes, I talked to both of them. Melissa said that she's going to be in town while we are visiting. I made plans to meet her in San Francisco, at her studio, but if I'm lucky I'll be able to get her to stay overnight at our place once as well," I said. "And Robert said that he and Crystal will be arriving at the house before us."

"Do we have a meeting time?"

"No, he made arrangements to pick up the keys from the Realtor and will leave our copy under the doormat. He said something about checking out the area while they are waiting for us. And he seemed to think that he picked out exceptional accommodations for our vacation this time."

"Given how picky Crystal is, I can only imagine that it will be pretty nice," he said. "Can you believe that he's been with her for over a year?"

"No, I figured he'd be with someone new by now. But I'm guessing that she'll insist on having the best bedroom again. That's for sure," I said, not wanting to remember Crystal's behavior during our last get together. "It's funny that their relationship is the one that's lasted the longest. I'm still trying to figure out what he sees in her, but at least he hasn't asked her to marry him yet."

"And how serious can he be if he's not at least thinking about marrying her?" Brad asked, with a twinkle in his eye. "Do you think that he'll ever marry anyone? He's been single and bouncing around from woman to woman for as long as we've known him."

"I'm not really sure if he's the marrying type. He's seemed really wrapped up in his career over the years," I said. "Although it's got to get depressing... defending those corporations against the sue-happy American public."

"Well, the money probably makes it bearable," he said, with a chuckle.

I had to laugh too. Seven years ago, after college, Robert had decided to stay and go to law school while the two of us had headed off to make our fortunes in the corporate world. We had chided him about remaining a poor student and he had called us business raiders, but now he was probably making more money than the two of us put together. Crystal, on the other hand, never really worried about working hard to make a living. She made it clear that she came from a well-to-do family in England and was pursuing a modeling career. During the time we had known her, she'd had some minimal career success, landing a magazine advertisement or two. But it seemed she mostly spent her days dieting, exercising and telling charming stories about the famous people she had met at this party or that event. When you saw Robert and her together, it wasn't really clear which of the two of them was the more socially desirable; they made a handsome couple and appeared to enjoy going to the same sort of benefit dinners and charity balls. He was always networking for new clients while she was showing off her beautiful persona and playing up her foreign credentials.

The dinging of the airplane's intercom speakers interrupted my thoughts and then I heard the captain introduce himself and the co-pilot. He then informed us that we were fourth in line for take-off.

After the stewardesses finished showing us how to inflate our life preservers, in the unlikely event that we would need them, Brad turned to me and asked very worriedly, "You didn't tell them that they could do the grocery shopping for us, did you?"

"No, are you kidding? We are going to make the dinner this time around. I don't even want to think about what Crystal would whip up for us."

Since college it had been a tradition with the three of us that we try out new meals and cook for each other. The last time we had all gotten together Crystal had made an effort to fit in by cooking us dinner. I'll never forget the look on Robert and Brad's faces once they tried a bite of her beef stew. I, myself, had never had anything quite like it before and couldn't figure out what was making it taste so bitter. Robert locked eyes with us over the table and had then been bold enough to ask her what she had put in it. She had proudly announced that she had made her beef stew out of liver and kidneys and eagerly awaited our favorable verdicts. Robert, always the diplomat, had told her that he had never tasted anything like it before. Brad and I were able to truthfully agree that indeed, it was unlike anything we had ever had before. For the rest of the meal I tried to concentrate on the conversation as I trained my mind to believe that this was probably some traditional English recipe that was eaten everyday by people on the other side of the big pond. We finished our meals and then were treated to party favors that included paper hats that we wore for the rest of the evening.

"I was thinking we could slow cook some babyback ribs and have coleslaw this time around," I said, reassuring Brad.

"Okay. Just as long as you make the whole thing low carbohydrate so Crystal can eat it," he said.

"Of course. I think that one of the best things about meeting Crystal has been learning her low-carb dieting trick. It was even worth eating that meat stew just to learn how she keeps her figure so trim. And maybe this time I can get her to teach me how to put on make-up," I said as I jokingly nudged Brad with my elbow.

"That will be the day."

Brad knew me so well. I never was one to wear a lot of make-up. It wasn't that I thought I didn't need it; it was just that I didn't like to take the time to put it on and then to be careful all day long to keep it from coming off. I wore just as much as I absolutely felt that I needed to. Maybe a little lipstick, mascara and some cover-up dabbed on my occasional blemishes or freckles. I generally wore my blondish-brown hair loose and it tended to go a little wild when I would forget to brush it. I kept my rounded figure trim, but I certainly wasn't model material. Crystal, on the other hand, always looked like she was ready to have her photograph taken; like she thought that today was the day she was going to run into a talent agent and be discovered. She carried a large handbag and was always digging into it, looking for something new to use to enhance her appearance. Truthfully, she was an absolutely beautiful blonde goddess, but for the life of me I couldn't figure out why Robert wanted to be with her. That is, why he wanted to be with her rather than with me. But that really wasn't a fair statement. He wasn't the one who had done the picking. It had been me, and I had picked Brad over Robert.

It had all started so long ago. I had grown up in Northern California but when it came time to go to college I decided that I wanted a big change. So I had applied and been accepted at an East Coast university. Deciding to attend meant that I had to pack up and drive off, leaving everything and everyone I knew behind. It was during that first week of school that I met the two men who changed my life completely.

The first time I saw Robert; it had felt like I'd been struck by lightning. I had been sitting on the grass in the main campus quad one afternoon, watching the marvel of fall-colored leaves being swirled by the wind and eating my lunch, when I looked up and saw him walk by. He was a striking figure, dressed all in black, on that sunny and warm autumn day. The color of his outfit matched his dark hair and he moved gracefully as he passed in front of me. When he was but a few yards away, he paused to check the time on his watch and I caught a glimpse of his brilliant blue eyes. Later I would discover that depending on what he wore his eyes were either an intense blue color or a deep green. I remembered thinking at the time that I didn't believe people could fall in love at first sight, but I was still convinced that he was someone I wanted to play a role in my life. As I pondered whether or not I should try to get his attention, I saw him turn toward the doors of the building nearest to me. I gathered up my lunch and backpack, following after him as quickly as I could, all the time thinking about what I would say when I finally caught up. After I entered the building, I found myself in a big open hallway with a large staircase going up, next to several sets of doors where many people were standing around as well as entering. I walked over to one of the openings and saw that they led into an enormous lecture hall. In it I could see students everywhere; some standing and others sitting down. I stood near the open doors, looking down into the room, searching for the black-clad figure I had chased, but I could not find him. As I stood there an older-looking gentleman, who I took to be a professor, walked in and wrote 'Chemistry 101' on the chalkboard in front.

"Welcome to Introductory Chemistry," the professor said. "I'm having my teaching assistants pass out the syllabus for this semester. Make sure that you get a copy before you leave. This course will be graded on the curve. That means that the average score will be a C grade, even if the average turns out to be ninety-five percent. It also means that, if the average score is a thirty-five, those people will also receive a C. So, you see, you will not be graded on your absolute knowledge, but rather on your knowledge relative to those sitting next to you. In this manner, you will not be penalized in the unlikely event that I lecture poorly on a particular topic. Please take your time to look at each of the students sitting next to you. Statistically speaking, only two of you will receive passing grades in this course, while one of you will receive something less than a C."

By this time most of the students had sat down in their seats and I was one of the few people in the room still standing. As everyone was examining the person on either side of them, I felt that my presence was too obvious. So I decided to leave. The next day, and for many days thereafter, I ate my lunch in the same place at the same time, but I didn't see him again.

Later that same week I met Brad. It turned out that we lived on the same dorm floor, but I saw him for the first time in the dining common. I had gotten a tray of salad, adorned with cottage cheese, and was looking around the dining room for a place to sit. I didn't know anyone and there didn't seem to be any places available where I could eat alone. As I began to get anxious about what I was going to do, I saw an attractive guy look up at me at just the right time; he smiled and then glanced down at the seat next to him, as though to indicate that he wouldn't mind if I joined him. He was of average build, had sandy-brown hair that he kept neatly cut and I noticed that he had bluish-hazel colored eyes. It didn't take me long to decide to take him up on the offer.

"Where are you from?" he asked as I sat down.

"California."

"Really? From LA?"

"No," I said. "Northern California. The rural, agricultural part. And you?"

"Boston area."

After a couple of hours we knew most of the basics about each other. I'd never felt quite as comfortable with someone as fast as I had with Brad. As the weeks passed the two of us became better friends. It was as though all the things that I had liked about my previous male friends were combined in him, without any of their bad faults. And after a couple of months went by we began to date because, as Brad put it, if we stayed friends too long we'd never be able to move on to a more serious relationship. As frightened as I was to lose our friendship, I gave it a try and found that things progressed smoothly over time.

It was during my sophomore year in college that I went to study at Brad's apartment and had the surprise of my life. Who would I find sitting at the kitchen table drinking a Coke? He was none other than the man that I had seen walking across the quad that afternoon, Robert. When he looked up at me and smiled, my heart stopped. I didn't have a clue what to say.

"Rob, this is Mary Ann, my girlfriend," Brad said.

"Pleased to meet you, my name is Robert," he said, getting up.

"Nice to meet you too," I said, sitting down at the table.

"Want a Coke?" Brad asked.

"Sure, make mine a diet though."

"Rob is helping me survive Organic Chem this semester," Brad said, handing me the soda can.

I opened my drink and began to include myself in their idle chitchat. The three of us ended up talking for hours and it turned out to be the beginning of a life-long friendship for us, and a small torment for me.

As the fates would have it, Robert was every much as interesting and attractive to me as I thought he would be. I kept waiting for him to say or do something that would make me not want to be with him, but he never did. He was always honorable in his dealings with women, had a sense of humor, and it turned out that he was a pretty good horseback rider and cook. He seemed interested in maintaining a friendship with both Brad and me, and just about every week the three of us would schedule things to do. Whenever he was dating someone we would make it a foursome rather than a threesome. I think that Brad and I may have scared off some of Robert's girlfriends, but he was always a good sport about it and whenever we gave the thumbs down to one he had offered up I noticed that soon she would be replaced with someone new. His manner and looks were good enough that he never had trouble finding someone willing to be his partner.

Sometimes Robert and I would spend time together, having heart to heart talks. And I was fine when we were alone. But whenever I thought about confessing my romantic feelings to him, I turned into a thirteen-year-old girl; tongue-tied and self-conscious. So I would concentrate on other things; giving him advice concerning his girlfriends, talking about his dreams. Then, when I wasn't with him, I would fantasize about how I would suddenly find the courage to tell him how I really felt and imagine what his reaction would be. But the next time I saw him I would again realize how foolish I was and keep silent about it. Instead, I knew all about his past, his hopes for the future and exactly what was going on in his love life.

While all this was happening, Brad and I took the next step in our relationship by moving in together. As our senior year began to draw to a close, we needed to make decisions about what to do. Robert had been accepted into a good law school, which is what his parents wanted for him. Brad was being badgered into starting a business in the Boston area by one of his classmates. Although he kept saying that he hadn't made a decision I knew he was giving it serious consideration because it would be a means for him to return home to his extended family. I, on the other hand, really wanted to go back to California, to pick up the life I had left behind and start working.

As I agonized about what to do, I decided that the best person to discuss it with would be Melissa. So I returned to the Bay Area during our college break and spent time talking about men, marriage and what the future would hold. I trusted Melissa's opinions because she had been my best friend since junior high school. We met when my family moved into a house a block away from where she had grown up. From the first moments we spent together it felt like we had known each other forever. And after a couple of years, her mother told me that Melissa had an imaginary friend named Mary Ann when she was little. Her mother felt that I was the personification of that friend; that Melissa had spent her childhood waiting for me to show up. And I had to admit that I, too, felt that our friendship had a magical quality to it. We took the same academic classes in high school, had the same friends, and dated the same men; at different times, of course. She was finishing up at UC Berkeley with dual degrees in Art and Art History. Her plan was to work at one of the San Francisco galleries, to make money, while pursuing her creation of art pieces. She generously offered me a place in her new apartment if I wanted to come home, but after a week of soul searching I decided to go back to college. I knew that I needed to resolve the issues that faced me there.

Once I returned and announced that I had decided not to move home to California, things with Brad went back to the way that they had been before. Only now he assumed that my plans obviously included marrying him once we graduated. He didn't discourage his relatives from helping us make plans for the wedding; an affair that we felt should be held locally so as not to offend either of our families, given that they lived on opposite sides of the country. Soon invitations were mailed to everyone. A beautiful outdoor location was picked and the day silently marched closer. As it did, the idea of taking my vows began to have the heavy weight of being a duty, rather than the joy of being the happiest day of my life. But I was surrounded by people who kept telling me how perfect Brad and I were together, and when I thought about it, I had to agree. We were very compatible; best friends with the same life goals. Brad was a person that I could easily go through life with. In fact, it was true that I wanted to see how his life turned out and to be a part of it. But no matter how hard I tried, I couldn't shake off my feelings for Robert. I desperately wanted to experience being held by him; to find out what having a fight with such a dynamic person would be like and to talk with him naked in bed during the wee hours of the morning after a night of passionate love making. The truth was, that while I 'loved' Brad, I was 'in love' with Robert. But, as fate would have it, Brad saw me as the passionate, determined woman I was, while Robert saw me as the ever-friendly girl next door. And as my wedding day approached my frustration with the situation grew and one night I became rather sullen and easily agitated. I was trying to get my mind off of the wedding by studying for an upcoming Economics test when Brad came into the room.

"My sister called this morning," he said.

"Really? What'd she want?" I said, looking up from my notes.

"She wanted to know if it would be okay, if Lucie could be the flower girl."

"Lucie?"

"You remember, her daughter, my niece. She's eleven and has been asking if she could be the flower girl," he said.

"But my little sister is the flower girl. I've already asked her. Your sister knows that."

"Yes, but she suggested that maybe you could make her one of your bridesmaids. She thought that might be more fun for her," he said.

"Is my eight-year-old sister also supposed to wear one of the strapless dresses that I picked out for the bridesmaids? I don't think that would be appropriate, do you?"

"Maybe not, but she also said that you might be able to pick something else for her to do. Maybe reading a poem or something?"

"Look," I said. "Even if I wanted to... there isn't really enough time to change things at this point. And my sister is looking forward to being the flower girl. I even bought the dress for her to wear already."

"I'm sorry, but I didn't think you'd feel this way. I sort of already agreed to let Lucie be the flower girl," he said.

"Without talking to me? Do you have any idea how upset my family is going to be about this? Do you have any idea how much work it is to set all of this up? Your sister knows. She planned a wedding. She's just trying to mess things up. I've had it... tell your sister to forget it. As a matter of fact, maybe we should all just forget it as well. I'm getting out of here," I said, picking up my purse and heading for the door.

Once I was alone I realized that I had built up a lot of angry energy and that I could possibly use it in a constructive manner. I decided that I wanted to go to Robert and finally tell him how I really felt, and to find out for once and for all how he felt about me before I got myself into a marriage that I might regret for the rest of my life. I reasoned that even if he turned me down flat, at least I would then be able to marry Brad without any nagging illusions. I had a head of steam and I was ready to find out what the situation truly was; how Robert really felt about me. I dug the keys out of my purse and drove my car over to his apartment.

I must have knocked on the door with firm determination because Robert answered the door with a quizzical look on his face. I could tell that he was in the middle of cooking dinner because he stood before me, cleaning fragments of food off of his hands with a wet paper towel. He took one look at me and seemed to sense my mood. He graciously invited me in, waving me to a bar stool next to the kitchen counter. I sat down and saw that he was sautéing some garlic in olive oil; without a word I had been invited for dinner and whatever else it was that I needed.

As I watched the garlic bubbling in the pool of hot oil I thought about what to say. I wanted to tell him that I had just had a fight with Brad; about how I had followed him that first day on campus to try to introduce myself; about how surprised I'd been to see him sitting at Brad's kitchen table a year later; how distressed I was to find out that he had become good friends with my boyfriend; and to explain how innocently things with Brad and me had started. Instead, I sat in silence as the garlic began to brown. I was mesmerized by Robert's perfectly manicured hands gracefully grasping the spatula that was slowly pushing oil around the skillet. I just wanted to scream, but all I could do was sit there in dumb silence. Finally, I broke the spell and went over to the stack of CDs in the living room. I asked Robert if he minded my playing some music and he indicated that it was okay. I put something softly soothing on and returned to my perch in the kitchen.

"Brad's sister wants her daughter to be the flower girl," I said.

"And…"

"I already asked my sister to do it. I bought her the dress and everything. She's looking forward to it."

"Maybe his sister didn't know that," he said.

"No, she knew. And she got Brad to agree to it already. I don't know what to do. I'm so tired of all this planning and dealing with our families. I just don't know what to do," I said. "I just had a big fight with Brad and I left."

"Wow. That's rough. But I'm sure that Brad didn't understand how important it was to you before he agreed. I'll bet that he fixes this somehow," he said.

"Well, I don't know how he can. We both have promised this to different people. I'm just sick of this," I said.

"You'll work through this somehow. Everybody I've ever known who got married had a rough time making wedding arrangements. I've never seen it fail. But you'll figure out how to make it work. I have faith in you guys," he said.

"You have more faith than I have," I said.

"Not really. I can just see things more clearly than you can right now. And remember, we're all under a great deal of stress right now. Graduating and making decisions about what we're going to do. I'm just trying to get ready for law school and dealing with all that. You guys are getting married, moving to a new place and starting a new business. You wouldn't be human if you weren't feeling some pressure right now."

"I guess," I said, looking somewhat glumly at the floor.

"Well… why don't you stay here until you feel up to talking to him about it? I have plenty to eat and no place to go tonight," he said.

"You're pretty popular, eh?" I said, smiling at him.

"Yes, always the bridesmaid, never the… oh, ouch! Didn't mean to remind you of…"

"No problem. I'm okay. And thanks," I said.

Somehow the fight didn't sound as dramatic to me when I told Robert about it as it had felt. And his response wasn't exactly what I was looking for, but I was very relieved that I could stay as long as I wanted that night.

During dinner I made half-hearted attempts to make the setting romantic. I got out two of his stemware glasses and poured some wine. I also turned down the lights and lit a couple of candles that I found lying in the drawer next to the cork opener. Although the meal was very pleasant, Robert appeared oblivious to my overtures. He talked of things like graduation and his fear of going to law school and becoming a lawyer. When we finished eating I suggested that we go for a walk. The night air was cooling off from the heat of the day and it was very pleasant to be outside. We walked down to the local park and sat on the grass under the stars, continuing to discuss mundane things. I found myself feeling more comfortable around him as I forgot that what I really wanted to do was tell him how I felt. This was how things always went; I mentally prepared myself to tell him how I felt, spent time with him, chickened out and then fell comfortably back into our role as good friends. Once I got settled into friendship mode I never felt that the time was right to disrupt the good time we were having together. And tonight was not turning out to be an exception to this rule.

Finally I felt chilled, as the night air turned colder, and I suggested that we get a cup of coffee. We headed to the nearby coffee house and ordered some decaffeinated java along with an ice cream sundae. I figured that if I wasn't going to be comforted by Robert's arms, I darn well deserved to be comforted by some hot fudge. Once we finished, we walked back to his apartment and when we got inside I plopped down on one of the two beanbag chairs in the living room. Again, I was contemplating if I should say something about how I felt. At the moment that the silence had gone on long enough to become uncomfortable, the phone rang. Robert got up and answered it.

He listened for a moment and said, "Hello Brad." Then he looked at me expectantly, "Have I seen Mary Ann tonight?"

I sighed and nodded my head.

"Wait a minute," he said, handing the phone to me.

Brad and I talked and I told him that I would be home shortly.

I hung up and thanked Robert for dinner. I wanted to reach out and touch his face but instead I found myself walking toward the door. I said good bye and began the long, sad trip home. As I drove I began to realize that I was not capable of leaving Brad without a justified reason. And as long as I was with Brad I could never admit my feelings to Robert. I had long suspected that Robert would think less of me if I revealed my feelings while I was still with Brad.

The drive took me past the park where Robert and I had just sat talking, so I decided to stop and take a moment to compose myself. I got out of the car and went to where, about an hour ago, I had been with Robert. Being there alone I could easily imagine telling him what I had wanted to say. It was then that I suddenly realized that I was never going to be able to tell him how I felt. I also knew that once I married Brad I would have to give up on the idea of trying to. I felt overcome by sadness and found myself sitting on the grass with tears rolling down my face. I didn't try to hide my sorrow because the park was about to close and I knew that I was alone. I just sat there crying, coming to terms with the fact that the possibility of having a relationship with Robert was disappearing with every day that passed. If I couldn't tell another man that I loved him because I had a boyfriend, I didn't think that I'd be any better able to tell him once I had a husband. My dream of being with Robert was coming to an end; while my marriage to Brad was actually having its beginning.

Consoling myself I remembered that, in some ways, Brad was the best thing that ever happened to me. We were best friends, had the same life goals and interests. I could envision asking Brad to join me in doing some of the adventurous things that I fantasized about accomplishing. I reasoned that I could do much worse when looking for a life mate. Of course, that didn't make the pain of walking away from Robert any easier. And at that moment, I knew in my heart that I had said good bye that evening to our ever having a more intimate relationship when I had walked out his door. I resigned myself to the fact that I was going to have to make the best of this situation and give up romantic flights of fancy if I wanted to have a happy marriage going forward. It was beginning to feel like being with Brad was my destiny and I tried to convince myself that things usually turned out for the best. Since I had been unable to tell Robert how I felt, there must be some cosmic reason for it. Once resolved, I felt a calm come over me and I returned to the car, continuing my journey.

When I opened the apartment door, I found Brad sitting on the couch waiting for me.

"Hi," he said.

"Hi," I said back, cautiously.

"I'm glad that I found you. I wanted to talk to you. I'm sorry for what happened earlier."

"Really? What exactly does that mean?"

"Well," he said. "After you left, my Mom called and I talked to her about how upset you got. She seemed to think that you were right, that I never should have agreed to let Lucie be the flower girl without talking to you first. She said that she's going to talk to my sister about it."

"Thank goodness," I said. "Because I was going to have to say that there is no way that I can tell my sister that she can't be the flower girl. But I don't want to upset your sister by backing out on her. Especially since we haven't really hit it off yet."

"Yeah, I know," he said. "But my Mom did mention one thing, if you want to think about it. Last year, at my cousin's wedding, they had two flower girls and nobody thought twice about it. My Mom suggested that maybe Lucie could be the second flower girl. And my family will pick up the extra cost of the dress; whatever you want her to wear, of course."

I thought about it for a minute, trying to imagine my mother and sister's reaction to such a suggestion. "That might work as long as my sister can walk down the aisle first," I said. "I'll talk to my family and see what they say about it. No promises though. They are under enough stress planning this whole thing long distance as it is. I just can't make it any more difficult for them."

"Fair enough," he said as he moved toward me, giving me a supportive hug.

After that, all was well in our tranquil domestic domicile and we never discussed where I had been or what I had done earlier that evening. And I was one step closer to becoming Mrs. Mary Ann Radcliffe.

I rarely saw Robert during the next couple of months and by the time the wedding day arrived, he was dating someone new. We were blessed with a beautiful summer day and had enough guests that I felt it was too many while Brad felt that there were too few. Upon reflection, it was probably just about perfect. We had two beautiful flowers girls who happily walked side-by-side down the aisle and eventually became the best of friends. Everything ran smoothly and when it was over we packed our things and moved to the greater Boston area, with me beginning the task of learning how to become a New Englander.

In three years Robert finished his law degree and moved to the West Coast to join a well-thought-of firm in Silicon Valley. We would continue to take vacations with him; either by himself or, as the years passed, with whichever girlfriend he was seeing. Generally we would get to meet each of them once because his relationships only lasted for six months to a year. Looking back, we got to meet a very diverse group of women. One was a real outdoors type and she would take him riding bicycles while dressed in tight lycra; another was quite prim and proper, she would dress impeccably in designer business suits for afternoon picnics; but my favorite so far had been the one from Texas, who had kept her accent and wore cowboy boots no matter where we were going. Some of her boots were dressy with rhinestones and some were more casual worn-out leather, but she had a pair for every occasion and I don't remember her ever wearing any other type of shoes.

Once Brad and I married, we stopped giving Robert negative opinions concerning his dating choices and I always tried my best to accept whomever he brought along. Although I never felt that any of them were as perfect for him as I would have been, I did encourage him to develop stronger ties with some of them. Then Crystal came along. Robert had been dating her longer than he had any other woman; over a year and a half by this time. I had tried to like her, but she never really made me feel comfortable. I had long suspected that she was seeing him for reasons other than being in love with him. I couldn't put my finger on exactly what I thought that she was up to; it could have been as simple as her wanting to marry well on the social scale. But I just didn't trust that she was going to put his interests on an equal footing with hers if they got together permanently. I never expressed my concerns to Robert about her and he had never talked to me about his feelings toward her. He would only tell me things about her that were facts; that she liked seafood or romantic movies if we were planning to go out. We never discussed more serious topics like whether she wanted to have children or not; even though I knew Robert felt at ease around children. I never heard him say that she treated him well or that he thought she was in love with him. His personal life with Crystal remained a mystery to me, but I hoped that she was less of an enigma to him.

To be fair, I had to consider that perhaps Robert's continuing interest in her was really the reason that I didn't adore Crystal. Was it was possible that I was just plainly jealous of her? I didn't want to think this of myself. I wanted to believe that I was happy with my decision regarding Brad and Robert, and I could truthfully say that I appreciated the consistent and orderly life that I had. Brad had not disappointed me in the husband department. He continued to be an attentive partner, occasionally trying to surprise me and always working to make me feel special. I remembered one Valentine's Day morning when he had to get up early to leave on a business trip. I had resigned myself to the idea that it wasn't going to be a very romantic day, but when I got up I found a heart drawn on the kitchen counter out of Hershey's Chocolate Kisses. In the center of it was a red rose in a vase and next to it a greeting card that said, 'I love you.' It was these thoughtful things as well as flowers arriving at random times throughout the year that made me feel that Brad cared about me and the status of our relationship. When I remembered how special Brad made me feel I didn't think that I had any reason to be jealous of Crystal; especially since I felt she wasn't very cosmically centered or happy herself. But perhaps I was fooling myself after all. Either way, given his history, it was entirely possible that Crystal would be gone soon from Robert's life. I knew I was going to be on the lookout for signals about the status of their relationship. It was going to be an interesting week.

As I was musing about how things might turn out, I heard the captain say that we were going to be landing shortly. He also informed us that the weather was mild and sunny in San Francisco. We landed without incident; got our bags and found our rental car on top of a parking complex. After we put our luggage in the trunk, I stood with my face toward the sun and deeply breathed in the warm salty air.

"What are you doing?" Brad asked.

"I'm smelling the air and feeling the sun. It feels like home," I said.

With every breath I took, I could feel the essence of who I was spreading throughout me. It was good to be back and I felt alive.

The baggage barely fit into the small trunk of the car because we had gotten a jazzy green convertible; its capacity for storage was a stark contrast to the roomy Sport Utility Vehicle that we drove at home. It didn't take long to figure out how to put the top down and then we headed for the crowded maze of freeways, toward the Golden Gate Bridge. I kept looking, hoping to see the bridge as we made our way across the city, knowing that we had to cross over several large hills before it would be in view. The memory of it was an image that I cherished when I was away. Finally, I could see the large orange bridge suspended between two points of land that jutted out into the bay before the ocean began. Even though we were in moderately heavy traffic, it didn't take long for us to work our way to it. Once we started to cross the bridge, I realized that the mile drive would be too short for us to appreciate its magnificence in full.

"Can we pull over at the lookout ahead?" I asked Brad, loud enough for him to hear me.

"Okay. Are you sure that there's someplace to stop around here?" he asked.

"Yes. Look up there," I said, pointing ahead to a place on the side of the road that looked like a parking lot.

"Got it. I'll get over in the right lane and pull over."

"Thanks. Can we also walk back over the bridge a bit? Do we have enough time?"

"I guess so. It's not like we are on a particular schedule. But I would like to get to the house in time to eat dinner at a reasonable hour."

He managed to navigate the car into Vista Point without incident and we began to walk back over the bridge, toward the city.

As we walked I remembered what I had been taught about the Golden Gate in my elementary school history classes. The bridge was an awe-inspiring structure that had taken four years to construct and had been completed in 1937. It had often been referred to as the 'bridge that couldn't be built.' Looking up today, we could see scaffolding hanging from the side and I smiled as I remembered that the bridge was always in the process of being repaired and repainted. I never could look at the bridge without conjuring up the image that I created as a child; it was that of the bridge being built with a large net strung under it, sort of like the apparatus that they used under trapeze artists. My mind had created this scene when I heard that they had actually strung a net while the bridge was being built. In reality, nineteen of the workers had fallen during its construction and were saved by it. They became known as the 'Half-Way-to-Hell Club.'

As we walked and looked to the left, we could see the skyscrapers in the financial district forming the outline of what most people considered to be the city of San Francisco. The walkway we were on was on the city side of the bridge so it was difficult to see much of the ocean when we looked to the right. Since it was a beautiful afternoon we had plenty of human company on the bridge, as well as seagulls flying overhead. Sailboats dotted the grayish-blue water of the bay between the Bay Bridge and us. I made sure to point out Alcatraz Island to Brad and told him of the time when I had taken a ferry out to the island and gone on a tour. I had learned that not only had Alcatraz been home to a maximum-security prison, but the island was also the location of the first lighthouse on the Pacific Coast. When we had walked about a quarter of the way back over the bridge I just wanted to stop and soak in the view before us.

The sides of the bridge, along the walkway, were surprisingly high. Even though I had seen them many times before, I was always surprised that I felt like I needed to stand on my tiptoes in order to even begin to look down. As I leaned over the edge of the bridge I felt Brad behind me. His arms came around me on either side and just gently held me. I relaxed and let my feet go flat against the ground. We stood quietly together and took in the expansive view. We could feel the world buzzing around us, but we were alone together making a memory that we could share. I had once read that the bridge had been built so that it could sway as much as twenty-seven feet in order to be able to withstand winds of up to a hundred miles per hour. It wasn't anywhere near that windy today, in fact, it was more like a stiff breeze but as I stood still, with my feet flat on the ground, I had the sense of a boat on calm water. And even though it was sunny, the air moving in off the ocean caused me to feel a slight chill. I wanted to return to the car and continue our journey, so we leisurely strolled the bridge walkway toward our car holding hands. When we returned I pulled my hair back into a ponytail and tied a scarf over it. With all the driving and walking my hair was beginning to make me look like a wild animal; not exactly the subdued glamour girl image I was going for. Once settled back in the convertible, we navigated north and began looking for signs that said 'Highway 1.'

CHAPTER 2

▼

"How far do we have to go before we reach the Highway One turnoff?" Brad asked.

"I'm not sure about the actual mileage, but I know that the exit isn't very far," I said. "And we need to stop at a grocery store, before we get on it. I want to pick up the food for tomorrow night's dinner, as well as some for the rest of the week. I think we're going to be remote enough that a quick run to a grocery store might not be an option."

"Agreed, but we're going to need to keep the stuff cold because Robert said it takes a few hours to get there. Let's pick up a chest and a couple bags of ice."

"That's an excellent idea," I said.

It didn't take long for us to find our exit, which was clearly marked. We got off the freeway and explored until we found a grocery store. It was easy to get the supplies that I needed; various spices, babyback ribs, flavored water, mayonnaise and shredded cabbage for coleslaw were a few of the essentials. Brad raided the nut aisle and bought a couple bottles of Napa Valley red wines, which we found were very reasonably priced. We also decided to pick up some cheese, eggs, lettuce, hamburger and four steaks in case we needed more food unexpectedly, although it was our general rule to eat out when we vacationed with Robert. That is, except for the one special meal that the designated cook would prepare. But sometimes we all felt too lazy to get dressed and travel somewhere, so an occasional impromptu meal would get made. We also managed to find a large chest and several bags of ice. After packing our supplies into the car we made our way back to the freeway and turned onto Highway One.

For the past several weeks I had tried to describe the coastline that ran along the highway to Brad, but no description could prepare him for the actual experience. It took us some time to drive through Marin County, where we couldn't see the coastline. Then we caught our first glimpse of the ocean. We went past Stinson Beach and continued through the Point Reyes National Seashore area. The road jutted inland for a little while and then came back to the shore at Bodega Bay. From this point on, the coastline would vary all the way from nearly being sea level to having magnificent cliffs that were hundreds of feet above the crashing waves below. We continued leisurely north taking in the afternoon sun and smelling the salt-filled air.

The road we traveled followed the coast surprisingly close at times. And it would curve dramatically, needing to be driven slower at some points. But slow was a perfectly delightful pace to go because all we wanted to do was look at the sights and take in the experience of the journey. Occasionally we would pull over to the right and let other cars, which were more anxious to go fast, pass us. These were probably local residents who saw this vista everyday and were more interested in getting to their destinations. We were tourists and content to make our trip into an adventure.

Finally we reached a part of the coastline where the waves were so far below us that we couldn't see them from the road anymore.

"Brad, could you please find someplace to stop here?" I asked, wanting to get out of the car and get a better look at the impressive view.

It didn't take long for him to find a reasonable place to park. I walked across the road toward the cliff side with Brad hesitantly following me. The coastline here was a series of little bays with land poking out on either side. Each one looked something like a half moon. We were near a point where the land boldly stood out in the ocean and when I walked out a bit onto it I was able to look north and see the outer rocks on the opposing jut and some of the cliffs closer to the road. I wasn't close enough to the edge of the cliff wall to be able to see the base below me. And even though I couldn't see the entire bay I was comfortable with how close I was to the edge. Wisps of my hair had worked their way lose from the scarf I had used to tie it back. But since I was facing the sea, they were being blown off of my face by the constant breeze.

The dramatic view of the surf hitting the rocks at the base of the vertical cliff was only a part of the experience that we had while standing there. In addition, the roaring sounds of the massive waves of water moving toward the shore being stopped abruptly by the immovable rock walls made me realize how really small and inconsequential I was standing there. There was also the feel of the microscopic fragments of water that became part of the air when they hit the rock wall below and were blown over it by the breeze. It sort of felt like there was fog, but the sun was shining brightly and there were very few clouds in the sky. These elements combined with the view made me remember that I was in a unique place on earth; a place that I had visited before when I was younger, and that had made the same impression on me at that time. Again Brad sensed that I was experiencing something profound and he quietly put his arms around me from behind, keeping a silent vigil with me.

I liked being touched by him and even though I was feeling more and more moist from the environment I also felt warm and serene being with him at this place. I turned around inside his arms until I faced him. My fragments of hair now blew around either side of his face and I smiled as we kissed. No cars were traveling down the road at this point so I had the feeling that we were the only two people alive on this desolate area of the coast. We then turned together toward the car and walked back holding hands.

When I reached out for the car door handle I noticed my camera on the back seat.

"Wait a minute," I said. "I want to take a couple of shots before we go."

I got out my semi-antique Olympus single lens reflex camera with its telephoto lens and retraced my steps back to where I had been. I took several photos with varying zoom settings. I was using black and white film that I would develop myself once I got back home so I also played with the light settings. When I finished the roll of film, I quickly made my way back to the road, but I had to wait for a couple of cars to pass before I could safely cross back to our convertible. I climbed in and we were again on our way north.

After a while the novelty of looking at the ocean wore off and I found myself looking at the houses that dotted the land on the right side of the road. As a child I had remembered them as being rather small and worn by the elements of the weather. As we drove along I saw many of the same looking buildings, but over the years it appeared that some new ones had gone up. Some of them were more contemporary in feel, with large walls of windows bravely facing the ocean so that their occupants would have a spectacular view. Brad had told me that the house we were staying in was one of the more modern-looking ones. It had been built about five years ago and was supposedly in very good condition with a breath-taking view. I was looking forward to seeing what it really was like. We had been driving now for a little over two hours and I was getting anxious to reach our destination.

Robert had told us that the house was located about a two and a half hour drive from the Sausalito turnoff and had described the mailbox that we would see as we traveled up the highway. We began to look for a bright blue box with a yellow daisy painted on it. Finally we were able to see something that looked like what we were expecting, off in the distance, and began to slow down. When we got close enough we verified that the number on the front of the box matched our paperwork and then I anxiously looked up the small hill to the structure perched upon it. The house was sort of an A-frame type structure. It had a point at the top, in the middle, with a gentle sloping roofline. The entire front of the house had large, nearly uninterrupted, glass windows. In front of the windows was a large walkout deck with a cedar railing. In fact, the entire house seemed to be made of cedar. The wood still looked fairly new, but you could tell that the house had been standing here for a few years. Overall, I was pleased by what I saw.

We turned into the driveway, drove the short distance up the hill and parked over on one side of the asphalted area next to the house. I got out of the car, grabbing only my purse, and found the entrance closest to where we were. I lifted the doormat and saw the key exactly where I expected it. It easily slipped into the lock and turned, so I opened the door and stepped into what obviously was the kitchen. Looking around I knew that it was going to be fun to cook and spend time in here. There was a center island that housed a stove and oven. As I ran my hand on the counters I realized, from the cool touch, that they were all granite. The island counter extended far enough out over the cabinets below, that bar stools had been placed underneath it, making it possible for people to sit and keep company with the cook. There was enough empty counter space on top that you could even comfortably eat meals there. The rest of the kitchen had beautiful cabinets and a gorgeous Santa Fe tile floor design. Looking left I noticed that there was a full-sized bathroom that ran almost the length of the back wall, interrupted only by another door leading outside to the back of the dwelling.

As I looked right, beyond the kitchen area, I smiled. There was a half wall with an entrance to the dining room area. Beyond the large table that stood in the center of that space, I could see that the entire far wall was made of glass and was facing the ocean. Even though we were a bit of a distance from the highway we had a spectacular view of the cliffs and the pounding waves below. I found myself drawn to the dining room glass window, where I just stared at the view.

"Wow… Robert wasn't joking when he said that this place has a great view," I heard Brad say behind me.

"Yes," I said. "With a view like this, I may never want to leave here to go do anything else this week."

No matter how the rest of the house was laid out I knew that I was going to enjoy being here. No longer concerned about whether or not our accommodations would be suitable I turned my attention back to my indoor surroundings. The dining area was separated from the living room area by décor, not physical walls. The glass windows stretched across the entire front of the house so, no matter where you stood, you could see the ocean view. The ceiling was two stories high, cathedral, accented with the same cedar wood coloring as the deck. There were two rooms upstairs that had a railing as one of their walls; they overlooked the dining and living areas, also having an ocean view. There was a sliding glass door on the side of the living room, providing access to the front deck and I made a note to go out there once I unpacked everything.

In the middle of the house, directly behind the living-dining area was a hall that turned into a staircase. At the beginning of the hall was a door off to the right side that went into a large-sized bedroom. It also had a sliding glass door out to the deck, which wrapped all the way around the house on that side. After noting that this bedroom didn't really get much sunlight once you drew the curtains over the sliding door, I made my way up the staircase. Once at the top, there was a landing with doors off to either side. I turned left, into the room over the kitchen, and found a large bedroom that overlooked the dining room area. I noticed that there were several suitcases in this room, with one of them lying opened on the bed. Several feminine shirts had been tossed on the bed with one on a nearby chair.

"I think I've found Robert and Crystal's room," I yelled to Brad, who was still checking out the downstairs.

I returned to the landing at the top of the stairs and, with a little hesitation, opened the door to the right. I was pleased to see that our room was approximately the same size as the other room, with the same view out the front window and overlooked down into the living room area. I looked to my left and noticed that there were two doors. One led into a walk-in closet, with what would be plenty of room for our clothing. The other one led into a bathroom. There was another door on the far end of the bathroom that gave access into the bedroom that Crystal had claimed. The bathroom appeared to be quite large, but I decided that if it turned out that there was a wait to use it, I'd rather make the journey downstairs and use that one.

"I think I owe Crystal an apology," I told Brad when he got to the landing. "They have the same size room as ours and I'd rather be over the unused bedroom than over the kitchen anytime because of the noise."

"That'll teach you to have evil thoughts about people before they do anything wrong," he said.

"We do share a bathroom with them though," I said.

"That could lead to some amusing moments," he said. "Well, I'm going to get the suitcases up here and the food into the refrigerator before that ice melts." With that he turned and headed back down the stairs.

I moved toward the glorious view in front of me and put one hand on the balcony rail. As my gaze turned downward I looked at the living room and noticed it was quite a way down and that the rail was more for show than function. I loved a good view but my slight fear of heights made me happy to be in contact with the wood when I was this close to the edge. Looking around I noticed that all the furniture in the house was either covered in creamy white leather or made out of teak wood that was very Scandinavian in nature with smooth, clean lines. It gave the house an uncluttered, but very inviting, feel. I also noticed all of the furniture seemed to be in very good condition, which I found rather unusual for a vacation rental property. I was beginning to feel that we had gotten quite a bargain as far as accommodations went this time. The sound Brad made, lugging our two suitcases up the stairs, interrupted my thoughts.

"Could you put mine on the bed?" I asked. "I'm going to grab my apron and get those ribs marinating so that we can have them tomorrow for dinner."

"Sure," he said, swinging my suitcase up onto the bed.

"I'll be right with you," I said, opening the case and looking for my apron. I decided to put the apron on over my clothes because they already felt pretty dirty from the plane trip and the drive up here. I was thinking that I would take a shower once I finished in the kitchen and at that point would put something fresh on.

I headed downstairs and out to the car to help get the groceries. It wasn't long until I was standing in the kitchen with a chef's knife ready to clean any unwanted bits of bone off of the ribs. Cleaning the ribs had to be the worst part of cooking them. I didn't mind making the barbeque sauce, marinating, or slowly cooking the ribs. But I rarely got lucky enough to find ribs that didn't need some sort of inspection with lots of bone fragment removal. These, thankfully, weren't too bad and I finished them quickly. I then pulled the translucent sheath off the back of them and began to heat up the ingredients for the sauce. I had been working on perfecting a barbeque sauce for several months. The world was full of 'famous' barbeque sauces, but I had finally found a recipe that I could make with artificial sweeteners that was unusual as well as good tasting. It was sort of sweet and sour with a hint of the traditional tang. I made it myself, rather than using a jar from the store, to keep the number of carbs low because all of us were watching our intakes. Soon the sauce was prepared and I wrapped the ribs in aluminum foil, along with the sauce, and put them in the refrigerator to marinate overnight.

Once I was finished with that, I cleaned the counters off and headed upstairs to take a shower. Brad had just taken one himself so I waited for him to towel dry and then I hopped in with my shampoo, conditioner and various soaps. It was a big relief to wash the feel of the airplane and remnants of salt water off of my face and body. I could smell the familiar and comforting scents of my usual toiletries. It had already been a long day and on East Coast time I'd normally be getting ready for bed. But the shower had invigorated me and I felt ready to take on the evening before me, and whatever it might bring.

When I was done I decided to put on a long tank dress. I had one made out of microfiber that hadn't wrinkled. I decided that a medium-sized pair of gold hoops would set the frock off nicely without looking over the top. Those along with my usual plain gold wedding band and watch should be enough for a casual evening out, which is what I thought that we had ahead of us tonight. I quickly ran a comb through my damp hair and used the blow dryer to take the rest of the moisture out of it. I knew it would remain straight until I went outdoors into the humidity and then my tendency toward naturally curly hair would take over. I also put some light powder on my face to even out my skin tones, some mascara on my eyelashes to give them some 'natural' length and then put some pink, flesh-toned lipstick on. After I slipped on some sandals, I was finished.

Feeling ready to leave, given a moment's notice, I then worked on unpacking all of our clothes; putting them in the closet and drawers. I decided not to unpack more of our toiletries yet and I went to retrieve my cosmetics and other things out of the joint bathroom. There would be time enough to arrange them once we decided how the sharing of the bathroom was going to go.

"You done up there yet?" I heard Brad yell up the stairs.

"Almost. Why?" I asked.

"Because I see a car coming up the driveway. I think Robert and Crystal are here."

"I'll be there in a minute."

Instinctively I looked in the mirror and ran my hands down my dress and then up through my hair. I wasn't excited by what I saw in the mirror, but I wasn't disappointed either. I took a deep breath and headed downstairs to wait with Brad.

Once I got to the kitchen I found Brad sitting on one of the stools, reading a newspaper that he had laid flat on the granite counter in front of him. I noticed that it was dated about a week ago, but figured that he was reading it to get some local flavor and pass the time while he waited for me. He closed the paper when he realized that I was in the room and we both waited silently for Robert and Crystal to come into the house. When we heard the doorknob being turned we gave each other a supportive look; we knew that other people were about to enter our well-structured, comfortable little world. The door swung open and Crystal entered, carrying several shopping bags, followed shortly by Robert. Both Brad and I said 'hi' to them in unison as they came in.

"Hi," Crystal said as she walked past us into the dining room and up the stairs to their bedroom. We could hear her footsteps above us on the floor as all three of us looked at each other in the kitchen.

Finally Brad broke the silence, "Hey Rob, good to see you."

Robert seemed glad for the distraction and responded, "Great to see the two of you as well. How was your trip here?"

"Not bad," I said. I tried to think of something else witty to say but came up with a blank. This was how it always was when I saw Robert again for the first time. I was back to being a teenage school girl with a crush that she couldn't handle or understand. I needed to quickly switch gears into the friend mode or I was going to make a complete fool of myself in front of everyone this weekend.

"The drive here from San Francisco was really breathtaking," I heard Brad tell Robert.

"Yes. We came up yesterday but it was overcast and a lot colder than it is today," Robert said. "Mary Ann, didn't you used to live here in Northern California growing up?"

"Yes," I said. "But we lived over the mountain ridge at the bottom of the Northern California Valley. I've been over here to the coast a lot, but didn't exactly grow up here." Good, I seemed to have my mental faculties somewhat back under control. "This is Brad's first time in this part of the state and I've been looking forward to bringing him here."

"Dragging me here is more like it," Brad said as he smiled at me.

"Robert, where did you guys go this afternoon while you were waiting for us?" I asked.

"We drove north to see what's up that way. Spent some time in the town of Mendocino looking through the shops and talking to the locals."

"Ah… that explains the bags of treasures that Crystal was carrying," I said.

"Yes, that explains the bags," he replied.

We then heard Crystal coming down the stairs. When she reached the kitchen I noticed that she had fresh lipstick on and looked as though she had run a brush through her hair.

"Bobby, did you tell them about the restaurant yet?" she asked.

"No. Not yet," Robert replied.

"Well, there's this quaint French restaurant about a hour up the road that sits out on the edge of a cliff. From what I could see as we drove by there must be a fabulous view of the sun setting every evening. If we leave now, we could probably get seated in time to see it," she said.

"Sounds good to me," I said. I could tell by the look on Brad's face that anything that involved sitting and eating would be fine with him.

"Great, let's get going then," Crystal said.

We all got our jackets and purses and made our way out to the driveway.

"Who wants to drive?" Crystal asked.

"Why don't you guys drive us," Brad said. "I think that we've been in charge of traveling enough for one day."

I was in total agreement especially since Robert was driving a large SUV that I could comfortably sit in and not have my hair blowing around in the wind, the way that it had in the convertible. We climbed into the backseat and waited for Robert and Crystal to get themselves situated up front.

As we began the drive up the road we were mostly quiet, looking at the view of the ocean as we went along. After a bit Crystal turned the radio on and we listened to an oldies station that played tunes from the Sixties and Seventies. As we watched the horizon of the water meet the sky I noticed that the color was slowly changing from a bright light blue into more of a yellowish-orange color. Finally we could see the restaurant up ahead and managed to find the entrance to it off of the road. We climbed out at the drop off area in front of the door and waited for Robert to park the car. He found a spot easily and joined us. We went into the restaurant foyer and asked for a table for four with a view, if possible. They didn't seem to be that busy and we were led directly to a table that was right next to a wall of uninterrupted windows facing the ocean. With all of these windows it would have been difficult to find a table without a view, I thought as I put my purse on the back of the chair and sat down.

We were handed menus and I quickly located something that was basically meat with a heavy cream sauce. That, plus vegetables, would make for a nice low-carb meal and I noticed that everyone else picked pretty much the same type of thing when it came time for us to order. Crystal had certainly made an impression on our eating habits over the past year.

"The sunset certainly is going to be spectacular here," I said. "Great place for us to eat our first night."

"I can't believe how orange the sky is getting and how beautiful it is setting over the water," Brad said.

The sky was turning a brighter and more intense crimson orange with every minute that went by. The few clouds that hung horizontally above the water were creating quite the display as the setting sun shimmered off of them. As I watched the show going on through the window I felt Brad put his hand on top of mine. With both of them resting on the table, I at first felt self-conscious, but then I realized that I shouldn't feel that way with my own husband. But I did feel that changing the conversation to something less romantic might be in order.

"So I marinated the ribs for tomorrow night's dinner if that's okay with everyone," I said as a conversation starter.

"That sounds really good to me," Robert said.

"Bobby, ribs? Nobody told me that we were going to have ribs. Are those like those strips of meat with bones still in them?" Crystal asked anxiously.

"Well," I said. "Actually yes, but they are babyback ribs so they are smaller and more tender than regular ribs."

"Do you put barbeque sauce on them too?" she asked.

"Yes, why?" I asked.

"Because I really don't like barbeque sauce," she said.

"Well, I'm not sure that you've ever tried anything quite like this sauce. I made it myself from a recipe that I found. It's more of a sweet and sour sauce mixed with a traditional barbeque sauce," I said.

"Well, that might be alright, but I've never had ribs before," she said. "What are you going to serve them with?"

"I planned on making some coleslaw, with a sugar substitute in it of course," I said.

"Well, that might be alright. But I don't really see why I need to eat something that I've never tried before. Do we have to have the ribs?" she asked.

"Don't you even want to try something new?" I asked. "I ate the stew that you made and I'd never had that before."

"You've never had beef stew before?" she asked.

Now I was in trouble. It was true that I had eaten stew before, but I had never had it made with organ meat. I tried to think of a nice way to say what I meant without getting into the particulars.

"Although it's true that I have had stew before I'd never had it made the way that you made it, with the English spicing and all," I said. I could feel both men at the table slowly becoming less tense as they heard my response. "If you're really not sure about the ribs, I suppose that I could cook you something else in addition to them."

"Well, what would you plan on cooking then?" she asked.

"Since we are right here on the coast, how about something with seafood in it? That is, if we can find a store on our way back from wherever we end up going tomorrow."

"I like seafood," she said. "Would you mind terribly if I pick up something too? I can make a salad if you don't mind."

"No, not at all. Would you like me to make you a low-carb salad dressing as well? I brought my personal recipe book along because it had the barbeque sauce directions in it. It would be no trouble to make us all a dressing to go with your salad," I said.

"That's fine, but I'm not sure if I'll make the salad or not. I'll let you know after we go shopping tomorrow."

Our conversation was interrupted at that point by our waiter delivering our meals to the table.

After we all made polite comments about how good the food was, Brad asked, "So what does everyone want to do tomorrow?"

"Mary Ann, are you going to be with us or are you visiting Melissa?" Robert asked.

"I was hoping to visit Melissa three days from now. At least that's what I proposed to her yesterday," I said. "Will that fit in with your plans?"

"We don't have any plans," Crystal said.

"Crystal's right. We don't have any firm plans, but I have a short list of things that I thought we could do," Robert said.

"What's on the list?" Brad asked.

"I was thinking that we could spend some time at either Stinson Beach or Muir Woods. Both are south of us. Or we could head up north a bit and spend some more time in the town of Mendocino where 'the Redwoods meet the ocean,'" he said.

"I'd be happy with any of those ideas," I said. "And I would add just spending time at the house, relaxing, to my short list as well. What do you want to do Brad?"

"Since I've never been here before, I'm game to try anything," he said.

"And you Crystal?" I asked.

"I don't care at all," she said as she ran her fingers on the water glass in front of her, making patterns in the condensation.

"Well then Robert, why don't you pick our first activity for tomorrow morning," I said.

"If it's okay with everyone, I've been meaning to go to Muir Woods since I moved out here. So that would be my first pick," he said.

"Okay, so tomorrow we'll go to Muir Woods, pick up some seafood and maybe salad makings on the way home, and then have dinner together," I said, feeling like I was becoming quite the social coordinator. I heard general sounds of agreement from around the table.

At this point the waiter came over, cleared our empty plates and then asked us if we wanted some coffee or dessert. We all decided to pass on the dessert, but we did order a round of decaf coffees and cappuccinos. By the time they arrived the sun had totally finished setting and you could see the glint of a full moon dancing on the ocean water.

"So what did the two of you do this afternoon?" Brad asked, after trying his coffee.

"As I told you, we went up to Mendocino," Robert said. "And I stopped in at the Realtor's office on the way. She had some interesting things to tell me."

"Really? Anything that pertains to the house that we should know?" Brad asked.

"Some yes and some no," he said. "One thing I need to tell you is that the owner meant to have the pool table out by now, but it's okay if we use it as long as we are careful not to scratch the felt."

"Pool table?" both Brad and I said in unison.

"Where is the pool table?" Brad asked.

"Didn't you guys go down to the basement yet?" Robert asked slyly.

"No, we didn't even realize that there was a basement," I said. "How do you get there?"

"There's a door in the kitchen that leads to the staircase. It's right under the one that goes up to the second floor. There's a pool table, as well as a bar. Complete with a TV," Robert said.

"Wow, I was so busy checking out the view that I didn't even open that door. I thought that it was a pantry or broom closet," I said.

Robert sat back in his chair with a smug smile on his face. "I guess if you didn't check out the 'broom closet' that you probably didn't bother to look out into the backyard either."

"No, what's out there?" I asked.

"Only a swimming pool and a 'small' guest house," he said.

"Only," Crystal said, "it's not that small. We were hoping that after you viewed it that maybe we could move into it." "Unless," she added, "you two want it."

I looked at Brad and he indicated that he didn't care either way.

"Well… I'll be happy to look at it, but I can't imagine that it could be better than the house. I just love the view and I've already unpacked our stuff. I think that we'd be happy to let you guys have the guest house no matter now nice it is," I said.

"Great!" Crystal said as she gave Robert a knowing look.

"So Rob, did the Realtor have anything else to say about the house?" Brad asked.

"She didn't say anything in particular about the house, but she did tell me something about the general area. This is something that Mary Ann will be interested in," he said, looking at me. "She told me that we should make sure that we take our cameras with us if we go up and down the coastline because sometimes you can see seals sunning themselves on the rocks beyond the surf. She said to make sure that you have a camera with a telephoto lens or zooming capabilities because it's hard to get really close to them. According to her, you really have to look to see them and that most people don't see them even when they are there."

"That sounds neat," I said. "I'm going to have to make some time to walk along the highway or however close to the cliffs as I can manage."

"Tell her about the trail down to the beach," Crystal said.

"Oh yeah, I forgot about that," Robert said. "She also told me that you can access one of the coves near us from the road. There is a sign posted with a pull-over area. However, there are two trails that lead down to a small beach. One is an old trail that is marked 'Observation Platform.' It does have a fairly good path out to a large deck, with fabulous views, about half way down the cliffs. It used to go all the way down to the beach as well, but that part forks off and has somewhat disintegrated over time. She recommended that we not use that, and to look for the new trail that only goes to the beach, it's clearly marked 'Beach' according to her."

"How far is it from the house and in which direction?" I asked.

"She said that it was north, and about a ten or twenty minute walk up the road. You can see the pullover for it from the house if you look," he said.

"That's great! I'm going to have to find it when we have some down time," I said.

"Just be careful if you do. The ocean is slowly eating away at the edge of the cliffs every time a wave comes in, according to her, and that old trail was made ages ago," Robert said.

"Don't worry... I have a small fear of heights so I won't be trying to pretend that I'm a graceful mountain goat or rock climber," I assured him.

The waiter brought the bill to our table, interrupting our conversation, so we decided to pay it and return to the house. The drive home was again a quiet one. I looked out over the inky black of the ocean that was only interrupted by silver lines made from the light of the full moon as the water moved. The darkness of the night again gave me a sense of how big a place the open ocean was and how small I was in the whole scheme of things.

When we turned into the driveway I tried to see the pool and guesthouse that were behind the main house. I then realized why I hadn't seen it before. There was a tall wood fence that surrounded the whole back of the complex and I had been so busy wanting to see the inside, and the view, when we arrived that I had just dismissed the wood wall and what might lie behind it. When we got out of the car we went inside and I headed toward the back door leading out to the pool area.

Leaving the house I noticed that the light from the moon combined with the outdoor lighting system made everything rather easy to see. There was also light coming from the walls of the pool, through the water, and more coming from a hot tub 'Jacuzzi' type of thing over to the side. Directly beyond the swimming pool I saw a medium-sized building that was styled the same as the main house and all four of us headed toward it.

As Robert searched through his keys for the right one he said, "The same key that works for the main house opens this door as well." With that he opened the door to the guesthouse. We all entered into what was essentially a very large studio apartment. There was one main area that had a bedroom set toward the back and a living room set toward the front. Again, there was a wall of windows, this time they overlooked the pool area and had an extensive set of light-blocking blinds that could be used for privacy. Off to one side there was a small kitchen area, big enough to make snacks, but not large enough to cook a dinner for four.

"This is pretty nice," I heard Brad say. "You guys should really be comfortable out here as long as this is where you want to stay."

"Yes," I said. "If you guys want to stay out here that's fine with us."

"Great!" Crystal said, giving Robert that knowing look again. I decided that she must have had a bet going with him about whether or not we would let them stay out here.

"Well, I better go get our suitcases out of 'your' house then," Robert said as he headed out the door.

"Sounds good to me," I said, slowly following him out of the guesthouse. I wanted to get a better look at the pool area. I kicked one sandal off and dipped my foot into the water. It was obviously heated and I decided that I was going to take advantage of it by doing some swimming while we were here. I then slid my other sandal off, picked them up and went over and stood on the top step in the Jacuzzi. The water was nice and toasty, but I had already figured that it would be from the steam that was rising. I was too tired tonight, but I intended to spend some time soaking in it while we were here.

As I stood in the water, I saw Robert hauling two large suitcases out of the house and I smiled at him.

"One more trip and I think we'll be out of your way," he said.

"You could never be in our way," I replied, wondering if he understood the true meaning of my words. He just gave me a smile and continued his task. After he dropped off the suitcases and returned to get the rest of the luggage, I followed him back into the house. He continued through the kitchen, but I stopped at the only unopened door remaining, my 'broom closet.'

When I opened the door there was only a dark space. I easily located the light switch on the wall beside me and turned it on. I could then easily see the staircase leading down and I stepped onto it. Once I reached the bottom I saw a large open space that was about half of the size of the entire first floor of the house with one wall of windows, again facing the ocean. It contained a pool table and a couple of Eighties arcade games as well as a bar area with a couple of couches and a TV. This part of the house had a more informal feel to it and I imagined that the previous tenants had spent a lot of their leisure time here. I looked into the liquor cabinet and saw that it was empty. Opening the refrigerator I found a good supply of ice cubes. I noted that they would be good to use in the ice chest tomorrow for our trip to Muir Woods. I then sensed that I was not alone in the room. When I turned around I saw that Brad had followed me down.

"Nice pool room," Brad said, looking around.

"Yes. I'm surprised that we didn't find it ourselves when we first got here."

"I think that Robert has all of their stuff moved out to the guesthouse by now."

"That's good," I said. "It's a rather unexpected stroke of good luck that we have the place to ourselves this vacation. I'm really happy with the set up here this time."

"Where are you guys?" we heard Robert demanding in a loud voice from the upstairs.

"Down here," Brad yelled back, toward the ceiling.

In a few seconds Robert appeared on the stairs. "I see that you found the pool table," he said.

"Yep, I finally found it," I said.

"Well, I've gotten all of our suitcases out of the upstairs and out to the guesthouse. I think that we're going to unpack and call it a night if that's okay with you guys," he said.

"Sounds great," I said. "We're still on East Coast time so it's way past our bedtimes."

"Yeah, that combined with being the married homebodies that you two have become, really puts a damper on your night life I bet," he kidded us.

"Well, you two single people try to keep the noise down out there as you party into the wee hours of the morning," I replied in kind.

We all chuckled and then Robert headed for the stairs. "See you in the morning."

"Yes, bright and East-Coast early!" I said.

I heard the backdoor close above me and I turned to Brad, "Boy, I hope that staying in the guesthouse makes Crystal happier than she was today."

"I'd agree with that too," he said. "I wonder what's bothering her so much. Maybe she was stressing over whether or not we'd mind them staying alone out there?"

"I guess it's possible, but if that's it then tomorrow she should be in a much better mood," I said. "On the other hand, whatever has her upset might not have anything at all to do with us; could be that she and Robert are fighting or that something back home is bugging her. Hard to tell at this point."

"It sure is," he said. "Rob seems to be in a pretty good mood though. I wonder how he's feeling toward her these days. This is, after all, the longest that he's stayed with the same woman since we've known him. Maybe it's getting serious."

"It could be. I've always wondered why he breaks up with his girlfriends after six months or so. Do you think that he gets bored with them or that he has a fear of commitment? Like maybe he's always going to be the proverbial bachelor?" I asked.

Brad gave me an odd look and said, "What makes you think that he breaks up with them?"

"I don't know why I thought that," I said. It was a very good question, however. I had always assumed that Robert moved from woman to woman because of either a fear of commitment or boredom. It had never really crossed my mind that these different women might have been leaving him for some reason. "Do you know something about these breakups that I don't know?" I asked.

"Nothing in particular or concrete," he replied. "But he once said something to me when we were alone that made me think that they all might be leaving him."

"Do you remember what he said exactly?"

"No, I don't. And anyway, it was more of a feeling I got from him. And I didn't want to pry by asking about it," he said.

"Umm, interesting," I said. Since I had never conceived of the thought that Robert's relationship problems were caused by something he was doing I began to reflect back about the different women he had been with. What possibly could be the common thread that would make each of them want to leave him after a certain amount of time? And, in contrast, what was it about Crystal that made her want to stay with him longer than the rest? As I tried to sort out what commonality the women had, I was interrupted by Brad's voice.

"I think it's time to go upstairs."

"Yes, let's make sure that the lights are out and that the doors are locked on our way up," I said, focusing my attention on the present situation.

"You want to lock the back door too?" Brad asked once we reached the first floor.

"Yes, I think so. Call me paranoid, but I like to know that the doors are locked when I'm sleeping and Robert and Crystal have a key to get in if they need to. Although I expect that they will be too busy to want to come over here."

"Okay, sounds good."

I climbed the set of stairs to the second floor and looked out the window beyond the balcony rail, transfixed by the view. It was a canvas of black with silver highlights from the moon on the water and it mysteriously pulled me toward it until I was standing right at the edge of the balcony. If I looked carefully I could make out some of the landmass, which was between the ocean and me, from the moonlight. But there weren't any manmade structures or lighting that interrupted the natural beauty of the scene.

"Don't turn on the lights," I said when I heard Brad coming up the stairs.

I could feel his presence when he entered the room and moved toward me. I felt his arms come around me from behind.

"Hi lady," he whispered in my ear. "Interested in something more that just looking at the view?" He moved my hair so that it was behind my ear and kissed my neck.

"Umm," I teased. "I don't know. What exactly did you have in mind?"

I could feel him fumbling for the buttons on the front of my dress and as he worked on undoing them in the dark he replied, "I don't know either. What do *you* have in mind?"

I tried to turn around to face him but he held me in place and said, "Not yet." I could feel him unlatch my bra in the front and then felt his hand touch my bare skin. He then used his other hand to turn my face toward him and he kissed me as I felt him gently touching me. He then unbuttoned a couple more buttons and slid my dress and bra down over my shoulders until I was standing in the dark, wearing only my underwear. I reached out for the balcony rail to steady myself as I felt his hands exploring my naked body. I turned toward him and put my arms around him.

"Let's go over to the bed," I whispered.

Silently we made our way to the bed and made love. Sex had always been something that was gentle and sensuous between the two of us and tonight was no exception. Brad and I had worked out a sex life that was satisfying to both of us, but we had spent many years together and sex was often very repetitive. But tonight had a certain spell about it. The new surroundings and the feeling of being part of the great outdoors, because of the view, gave our union an excitement that had been missing in the last months. I was dead tired, but the slow love making was keeping my interest tonight and I found myself feeling very content and bonded with him.

When we had finished we both put pajamas on and climbed into bed. After I pulled the covers over myself I felt Brad in bed behind me. He put his arms around me and I closed my eyes. I could tell that I'd be asleep shortly.

CHAPTER 3

▼

When the sun came up the next morning I discovered the main disadvantage of living in a house with a fabulous view. The morning light streamed in from the front wall of windows, and even though they faced west it was still bright enough to wake me up. Since I was still on East Coast time I wasn't that distressed, but I made a mental note to myself in case I ever entertained purchasing a house constructed with a lot of glass. Once I fully opened my eyes and sat up in bed I found that I was once again mesmerized by the view. I could see some wisps of morning fog lying low to the ground, but I knew that soon it would burn off. Beyond that the sun was brightly glinting off the water and the ocean seemed to extend into infinity. When I reached over to Brad's side of the bed I realized that he had already gotten up and then I heard some noise from the downstairs.

"Brad, is that you?"

"Yes, it's me. And I've got the coffee made too."

"Excellent," I said, rolling out of bed. "Do you know what time it is?"

"About seven-fifteen."

"Boy, did we sleep in today. It's really ten-fifteen back at home."

"Well, some of us slept in. I've been awake for over an hour."

"Am I the last one up?" I asked, cautiously looking over the balcony.

"Nope. Not that I know of," he said. "I've been down here by myself. Haven't heard a peep out of our 'guests.' But I guess that they could already be up and hanging around out there."

I grabbed my robe and put it on. As I tied its sash around my waist, I checked myself in the mirror. I decided to run a comb through my hair and brushed my teeth, just in case Robert and Crystal showed up. Finally feeling semi-human, I headed downstairs to get a cup of coffee; its aroma had been beckoning to me from the moment I had woken up. I saw that Brad had gotten fully dressed and was again reading the same newspaper from the night before.

"Cream is in the fridge," he reminded me.

"Thanks, I'm in the mood for dessert coffee this morning."

I found a large mug in the cabinet and filled it with coffee, sugar substitute and a dollop of cream from the carton that I located in the refrigerator door. Then I sat down at the counter next to Brad, "Any interesting information in that old paper?"

"Not really. I'm mostly just thumbing through the classifieds, to see what the real estate market is like, what kinds of junk people are selling and also getting a feel for the job market. I'm just waiting for everyone to wake up so that we can get this show on the road."

"I see. I still need to shower and then we all should have breakfast before we leave," I said, holding the warm mug between my hands. "But I'm not doing anything until I finish this cup of coffee. You don't think that they are making breakfast out in the guesthouse, do you?"

"Don't think so, since they didn't move any groceries out there last night."

"Okay then. I'll take my shower in a minute."

I left Brad with his newspaper and sat down at the dining room table. I wanted to watch the waves pound against the cliff walls while I savored my morning cup of decaf. As I sipped my coffee I began to wonder about what Brad had said last night. Was it possible that Robert's girlfriends had broken up with him and not the other way around? As I thought about it, I realized that over the years I had put Robert on something of a pedestal. I rarely ever thought anything negative about him. To me, it had been nearly inconceivable that any woman would find his behavior objectionable. Thinking about it now, I came to the conclusion that no one could be that perfect and that Robert must have some flaws. But in my mind, I just saw him as having many charming personality quirks. At times he would joke around about things that were personal in nature, but I always thought he did that to put people at ease. He was never shy when it came to giving his opinion about what he wanted to eat or what he felt in the mood to do. Although that could be perceived as being demanding, I always liked the fact that he never hid his feelings.

Through the years I'd learned to depend on his consistent behavior and I enjoyed his apparent self-confident way of saying what he really thought. Further, I wondered how anyone could not help to see how loyal and honorable he was. I remembered that night when I'd gone to his apartment and how easily he could have taken advantage of my confusion and how, instead, he had helped to steer me through that night so I didn't have anything to regret the next morning. On the other hand, it was possible the women he attracted didn't like these qualities or perhaps living long-term with these characteristics was more difficult than it looked. It might even be that he responded differently when he was involved with someone in an intimate relationship; after all, no one really knows what any two people's relationship is like when they spend time alone. Perhaps Robert turned into someone I didn't know once he partnered up with them. I made a mental note to keep track of what went on between Robert and Crystal. Perhaps the way they interacted would give me some clues or provide proof that Brad had been mistaken.

I finished my coffee and decided that I had time to make salad dressing, for tonight's dinner, before showering. I quickly flipped my recipe book open and got out the spices, mayonnaise and sour cream. I dumped the ingredients into a small bowl, mixed them with a spoon, then covered it with plastic and put it in the refrigerator so the flavors would intensify.

"I'm going to take a shower now," I said as I closed the refrigerator door.

"Okay," Brad said, continuing to read.

I went upstairs and got the shower running. When I finished, I put on a tank top with a pair of capri pants and then went through my morning ritual of combing my hair and applying a touch of makeup. I grabbed a pair of sneakers because I knew that we'd be doing a lot of walking if we were headed to Muir Woods and I wanted to be comfortable. Then I remembered that the shade from the trees made the paths cooler so I located a light cardigan and tied it over my shoulders. Short of some freak weather situation I figured I was ready for anything the day had to offer. As I headed downstairs I heard voices and realized that Robert and Crystal had finally arrived and were talking to Brad. I hurried to the kitchen and found everyone standing around chatting.

"Morning sleepyhead," Robert said. Usually I was the last one up and it was a running joke between us whenever we vacationed together.

"What are you talking about? I've been up, waiting for you guys to get up. I've had coffee, made salad dressing, contemplated the universe and even taken a shower," I replied. "Have any decisions been made about what we're doing about breakfast yet?"

"Nope, we were just talking about that," Brad said. "I think the general consensus is that we stop and get something on our way to the woods, unless anyone is really hungry now."

"I'm not really hungry right now, but I will be in a couple of hours," I said. "Have we decided if we want to just go to the woods or do we also want to try to hit one of the beaches down there as well?"

"I definitely want to spend time at the beach," Crystal said.

"Fine," I said. "How about we get breakfast, go to the woods, decide about lunch, go to the beach, get some groceries and then come back here and I'll make dinner?" Yes, I definitely was earning my stripes as the social coordinator this week.

"That sounds good," Crystal said. "But I'm not very hungry so maybe we don't need to have any lunch. I'm not really that interested in breakfast either."

"Let's just see how it goes," Robert said.

I knew Brad and I probably didn't need three meals today either, but I definitely was interested in some breakfast as well as some more coffee. I found an old travel mug in the cupboard and filled it with decaf for the road.

"We still need to get our swimming suits and towels together for the beach," I said.

"So do we," Robert said. "Why don't we meet by the cars in a couple of minutes?"

"Robert, don't forget the suntan lotion," Crystal said.

"I'll remember," he said, walking toward the door.

As I started to leave the room I noticed Crystal was wearing a short sundress and a pair of strappy sandals.

"Crystal, you might want to consider putting on some comfortable shoes. My memory is that the wood trails are long so we're probably going to be doing a lot of walking."

"Oh, I'll see if I have some proper shoes," she said.

When I saw her again by the cars I noticed that she was still wearing the sandals, but figured she had stowed a more sensible pair in the oversized tote bag that Robert was carrying.

"So, how do we want to handle this?" Brad asked.

"How about we head down Highway One, south, until we see a café or something else?" Robert said. "If you guys have a cell phone we can call each other once we spot something."

"Sound good to me," I said. "We have a cell phone. And I think that I remember a breakfast-looking place about half way down the coastline, maybe a little further. It was in a small town and was colorfully painted pink, yellow and blue."

"I think that I remember that too," Robert said. "Is your cell number the same?"

"Yes," Brad said. "Look's like we're all set."

"Okay," Robert said, as he put the tote on the back seat of the SUV. "Let's get going and whoever sees a good breakfast place first calls."

We ended up following Robert and Crystal back down the highway. On this trip I was a little more anxious because, as the passenger, I was the closest to the ocean side and it felt like I would fall straight down the cliffs if I took one step out of the car. At times the road seemed to barely have enough room cut out of the side of the mountain, and I was getting a much better view of the sheer drop from where I was. Often we went too close to the edge for my comfort, but the view was breathtaking once I got over my fear. I didn't talk much to Brad because I wanted all of his attention on the road while he was driving.

It didn't take long for the sun to burn off the fog and it was clear that we had the makings of yet another beautiful day. As we wound our way back down the coast I became a little concerned when I noticed that the cell phone wasn't getting a very good signal. Thankfully, once we reached the little café that I remembered, I saw that Robert had already pulled off the road into the parking lot.

After a short meeting we all agreed that this looked like a decent coffee and omelet place. Given that it was a weekday, we didn't have long to wait for a table and soon we were picking out our breakfasts. We all ordered omelets with various meats, cheeses and vegetables except for Crystal, who ordered just a couple of scrambled eggs. When the food arrived I noticed she didn't eat much. Robert noticed her lack of appetite as well.

"Crystal, is there something wrong with your eggs?" he asked. "Want to order something else?"

"No Bobby. It's like I said, I'm not hungry after eating that large dinner last night."

The omelet I ordered was generously sized and I felt full, but after spending a morning walking around in the woods I figured Crystal was going to want some lunch. Once we finished eating we plotted a course to Muir Woods on our maps and agreed that if we got separated, we would meet at the main entrance. And again we were back on the road, Brad following Robert.

Soon we were parked in the lot at Muir Woods. I noticed that Crystal was still wearing sandals and thought about reminding her to change, but then decided saying something to her once was probably more than enough. I didn't want to be seen as the nagging mother of the group. We found the Visitor's Center and picked up some trail maps. After reading through the descriptions I noticed there were easy trails that would only take an hour or so to complete as well as really difficult trails that would take at least half a day to walk.

"There seems to be quite a bit of difference in which of these trails we might want to take," Brad said.

"Yeah, I see that," Robert said. "I'm up for one of the half-day trails if the rest of you are, but I don't want to do the most difficult one."

"I'm glad to hear that," I said. "According to this guide, the hardest trail has a direction sign for a portion of the trail that you're supposed to ignore unless you want to hike over terrain that's steep, dangerous and has an erosion problem."

"That sounds simply delightful," Crystal said, as she folded the trail map and put it into her outer purse pocket.

"Don't they ever fix anything that's eroding out here?" I asked jokingly, remembering our conversation from last night.

"Guess not," Brad said. "I'm up for the Bootjack Trail to Ben Johnson Trail Loop if the rest of you are."

I liked the way those trail names sounded. I looked in the brochure and found they were moderately difficult ones that would take about three and a half hours to complete. "I could handle that. I'm up for it too."

"What about you Crystal?" Robert asked.

"I'm not really up to a half day hiking. I think that I'd rather do the main trail to Cathedral Cove," she replied, and then continued to apply the lipstick that she'd fished out of her purse.

"Well, that's a very easy trail, and only takes an hour. I had something a little longer in mind if you can handle it," he said.

I looked at my map and found a possible solution, "Hey, we could add the Hillside Trail on to the Main Trail and maybe that would work."

Robert looked at his map, "Crystal, would that be okay with you?"

"I guess so," she said, capping the lipstick tube and dropping it back into her pocketbook. I didn't think she looked too happy or thrilled with the compromise.

"It will be pretty easy," I said, trying to reassure her.

"We should buy some bottles of cold water before we get going," Robert said.

"Great idea," Brad said.

I stayed at the car, while they went off, and took all of our swim gear out of my backpack so that I wouldn't have to carry the extra weight. I checked my camera and made sure I had film loaded. I decided to wear it around my neck; making it convenient to get to when I wanted to take a photo. Once satisfied that we had everything, we started down the trail. Since there would be plenty of time to finish the hike I took my time, reading the different informational signs that were located next to the fauna and other points of interest. A few people walked along the path with us, but I noticed they were talking in hushed whispers so as not to disturb the quiet of the natural setting we found ourselves in. I, too, was feeling very peaceful in my surroundings, except for the tension I was feeling between Robert and Crystal.

The trees were absolutely gigantic. I spent the first quarter of an hour or so just looking up at them, towering over me. Most of them reached up hundreds of feet and were so dense that you really couldn't see any sunlight at all coming in between them. Most of the undergrowth we saw was foliage that didn't require sunlight and liked moist surroundings. Things like big, beautiful ferns and plants whose Latin names I couldn't pronounce very well. I had brought the sweater thinking that I might feel a little chilly without the sun shining directly on me, but I found I was comfortably warm instead. We had picked the perfect day to make this journey.

After a while I noticed we seemed to be drifting away from each other, into couples. Brad and I were interested in reading the placards for the various plant life, while Robert and Crystal seemed to be having a conversation quietly between themselves. Brad seemed totally oblivious to what was going on and reached over to hold my hand. I, too, tried to concentrate on Brad, but my attention kept getting pulled back to what was happening with Robert. I saw them talk for a while and then Robert handed Crystal his cell phone. I expected her to make a call, but instead she slipped the phone into her purse and the two of them rejoined us. I didn't think anymore about it until we reached the second bridge. There Robert announced that Crystal was tired and was going to cross over to go back to the Visitor's Center and wait for us.

"Yes," she said. "I guess I should have taken Mary Ann's advice to wear my sneakers because my feet are beginning to kill me. I'll just wait for you guys and then we can go to the beach."

"She's got the cell phone in case she needs to call," Robert said.

"I see," Brad said, looking at his watch. "It should take us about another hour or so to get back. Crystal, try to find someplace comfortable to wait. If we don't find you when we get back we'll give you a call."

"Thanks," Crystal said. "I'll just go and wait for you guys. Enjoy the rest of your hike." We watched her cross the bridge and walk around a curve in the path until we couldn't see her anymore.

"Was it something we said?" Brad asked Robert once Crystal was out of sight.

"No. Not really. She's just not that excited about doing outdoor things."

"If you want, we can cancel the beach this afternoon and do something else," Brad offered.

"No, she's really looking forward to going to the beach," he said. "At least I think she is."

"Let us know if she doesn't want to, okay?" Brad said.

"No problem, I'll check again with her when we get back," he said.

"Okay, then let's press on," Brad said.

When we began to walk, I noticed that we had picked up our gait. I wondered if we were moving along because we felt an oppressive force was gone or if we were hurrying to finish our task of seeing the woods. After a few minutes Brad and Robert started reacting to each other the way they had years ago, when we were all in college. Soon the three of us were back to our old ways of interacting and joking around. I had always found it interesting that the three of us could be comfortable as friends. Although Brad and I were always the romantic couple, Robert never acted like he felt he was a third wheel. Our system of friendship was more like a rotating odd-man-out game, where two people would take sides against the third and then one of the two would side with the lone one and make fun of the next in turn. As we made our way through the woods, all the tension I was feeling disappeared. I felt happy that we could so easily fall back into our old patterns, even with the passing of the years and our diverse experiences apart from each other.

As we continued on I noticed some of the other visitors in the woods were giving us stern glances and I realized we were making a bit more noise than everyone else. I cautioned my companions and we tried to keep our conversations down to hushed whispers, in between giggles and laughter. A little further along we saw a family stopped and staring off into the woods. When they heard us approaching the mother turned to us and put her finger to her lips in a silent 'be quiet.' She then pointed into the forest as if to direct our attention there. We quietly walked to where they were and finally saw what they were looking at. About twelve feet off of the path there was a mother deer with her baby. The mother was lying in the ferns while the little one was practicing how to walk. We stood there watching them for a few minutes when finally the doe seemed to notice that she and her fawn were drawing quite the crowd. She got up and slowly walked further into the woods with her offspring trotting cautiously behind her. We all stood still, in silence, watching. Then I remembered I had my camera hanging around my neck and I wished that I'd had the presence of mind to pick it up and click a photo or two. I'd never been that close to any deer before, much less one that was nearly a newborn. Once the two of them disappeared into the darkness we finished our walk, but with a little less frivolity and joking around.

At the end of the hike we easily found Crystal near the Visitor's Center, sitting at a picnic table reading a book. She seemed indifferent to seeing us and made remarks about how fast we had been and how she had expected it to take us much longer to finish the trail. She also pointed out that her shoes had given her a blister and that she had found a bandage to put on it. Brad looked at me and I knew he wanted to leave Robert alone with her so that he could find out what she wanted to do for the rest of the day. So we walked out to our car and began organizing our swim things back into our pack. We were nearly finished when Robert and Crystal joined us.

"Would it be okay with you guys if we skip lunch and go to the beach, and then swing by the grocery store before we return home?" Robert asked.

"No problem with that," Brad said, while I nodded in agreement.

Once we agreed to her plan, Crystal got into their car. Brad pulled a map out and consulted with Robert about the route. After they decided to meet at the entrance of Muir Beach, we returned to our cars and headed off independently.

Alone in the car with me Brad said, "I didn't want to say anything, but I really could use something to eat. If we see someplace, let's grab something fast. I'm willing to eat almost anything."

A short distance down the road we saw a mom and pop's fast food stand. We pulled over and Brad got a burger and fries. I was still full from breakfast and knew I could easily go without eating for the next six or so hours.

"Brad, why don't you let me drive, while you eat, so we won't be too late meeting Robert and Crystal," I said.

"That would be great," he said, opening his bag of food as he slid into the passenger seat.

Shortly after Brad finished we spotted the entrance to the beach, as well as Robert's car. We waved and then followed them into the parking area.

Once we all got out, I saw Crystal was in a much better mood. She had grabbed the tote with her beach stuff and was eager to go change. I got our backpack and handed Brad his suit and towel. Then we paired up and Crystal and I looked for the women's changing room.

Once we were alone Crystal said, "I've definitely decided to make a salad for dinner tonight."

"That's fine with me," I said.

"Great. And I hope you don't mind if I bring along a dressing as well."

"Not at all. I made a garlic ranch dressing this morning, but it's fine if you want to bring another one."

The dressing rooms weren't very crowded and I easily found an empty stall with some privacy. I put on my one-piece swimsuit and then I threw on some capri pants as well as my camp shirt, unbuttoned, over it. I had some rubber thongs, so I slid them onto my feet as well. Although I was in fairly good shape physically I still didn't feel comfortable wearing a bikini, especially when I compared myself to Crystal. I imagined that she brought a very revealing swimsuit and if I had her perfect body I might be tempted to wear such a thing myself.

A couple of minutes later, when I saw Crystal, I had to smile to myself. Her choice of swimwear did not disappoint me in the least. I knew that she was going to have every man's attention when she walked down to the beach. She had picked the smallest bikini that still managed to cover the most intimate areas of her body. And she looked absolutely fantastic in it. Her body was well tanned, either from a bottle or from some form of tanning sessions, and every curve was pure perfection. I truly couldn't imagine that any form of plastic surgery could have improved how she looked. I would have felt jealous, but I just remembered that looks weren't everything and reminded myself, that in the whole scheme of things, I was comfortable with myself.

We found Brad and Robert, waiting for us outside of the dressing rooms. Since it was a beautiful, temperate day the beach was already pretty crowded, but we found a patch of empty sand and put our towels down.

"Bobby, could you help me put this lotion on my back?" Crystal asked.

Robert dutifully picked up the bottle and began to squirt the lotion into his hands.

"Mary Ann?" Brad asked. "Do you want to walk with me?"

"Sure," I said. "I'd love to try to find some shells to take home as souvenirs."

I was happy to go off with Brad because one of my favorite things to do when I visited the sea was to look for any treasures that may have washed in. And I was beginning to get the impression that Crystal was happiest when she was alone with Robert, rather than being with all of us.

We spent over an hour walking and chasing each other through the waves. When we returned back to our towels, both Robert and Crystal indicated they were pretty toasted from the sun and ready to leave. This fit well with my plans because I still had dinner to cook and we all had shopping to do. It didn't take Brad and Robert long to plan our path home and to pick which grocery store to stop at. I was happy we were all going together because I wanted Crystal to help decide which type of seafood I would buy. We changed back into our street clothes and were on our way. Once in the grocery store, I dragged everyone to the seafood section.

"Crystal, they have a number of things here already prepared. Is there anything that you would like me to buy?" I asked.

Crystal looked at the boxes of frozen seafood dishes, "I guess anything would be fine."

"Is there something you like in particular?" I asked.

"Not really. I haven't had that much seafood so I don't really know what I like," she said.

"How about you Robert?" I asked. "Is there something you like that I could make? I'd like to try to stay with the prepared stuff, if possible."

"Crystal, how about the crab cakes?" he asked. "The last time we had crab cocktails you seemed to like that."

"You're right Bobby, I did. I guess that would be okay."

"Mary Ann, the crab cakes will be fine," he said, pointing to the freezer section where several brands were located.

"Fine, I'll look at them and pick out something."

"Bobby, I need to get vegetables for my salad," Crystal said.

"Yes. I know," he said. "Why don't we meet up with you guys back at the house once we finish our produce shopping?"

"Sounds good Rob," Brad said. "See you then."

When Brad and I were alone I looked at the ingredients on the boxes and picked a brand that had very little filler, a low carb count, and easy directions for preparation.

"That was odd," I said.

"What was?"

"Crystal and the seafood thing…"

"What do you mean?" he asked.

"I distinctly remember Robert saying Crystal liked seafood the last time we were together. Remember how we had to try out that trendy new restaurant?"

"Vaguely… That's right. She wanted to go there because she liked seafood."

"Exactly. Well, hopefully she'll like these tonight," I said.

We spent a little more time shopping for a few things I might need and then drove uneventfully back to the house.

We were the first to arrive and I headed directly into the kitchen and put the ribs in the oven so they could begin slow cooking. Since I had a couple of hours to wait I began to busy myself making coleslaw and setting the table. The dishes that were in the cupboards weren't the fanciest ones I'd ever seen, but they went nicely with the teak table. I found a vase under the kitchen sink and I put a bunch of wildflowers I had purchased in it. It served well as a centerpiece. When I finished, the overall effect was simple elegance and I was satisfied.

While I was working, I heard Robert's car pull up outside in the driveway. When they didn't come into the house I figured Crystal must have decided to prepare her salad in the guesthouse. I was somewhat relieved to have the kitchen all to myself, but once I finished getting everything ready I began to wonder why they still hadn't come over to join us. What was taking her so long to cut up a head of lettuce and slice up some vegetables?

"Brad?" I asked.

"Yes?" I heard him say from the living room.

"Once you get ready, could you go over and let Robert and Crystal know that dinner will be ready in about an hour and a half?"

"Sure, I'm set to go now."

I headed upstairs to put on a simple dress with some tasteful jewelry and by the time I finished Brad had returned.

"Rob says to tell you that they are almost done getting ready for dinner and will be over shortly," he said.

It didn't take long until we heard the back door open and saw both Robert and Crystal entering the house. I was somewhat surprised at how Crystal was dressed. She had put on a formal short black dress, had totally redone her make-up and hairstyle. She looked like she was ready to go out night clubbing in the city. I, on the other hand, had just put on a clean dress and looked like I was ready to stroll through a well-manicured garden carrying a straw hat. Both of the men had dressed in nice casual clothes, a pair of Dockers with a polo shirt, Robert in darker more formal colors and Brad in lighter, less formal ones. Robert came carrying two bottles of red wine and he poured a glass for both Brad and himself. Crystal and I opted for diet sodas with ice. After the drinks were made we sat in the living room and talked about current political events as well as recent sport scores. The time passed by quickly, with the men doing most of the talking. I enjoyed being around the two of them and Crystal appeared to just want to listen to them as well.

Finally it was time to finish preparing the meal and get the food on the table. I excused myself from the group and located the crab cakes in the refrigerator. The instructions called for them to be cooked with butter in a skillet. I busied myself checking on things while I waited for the pan to heat up. When I took the food out of its container I noticed that Crystal had joined me. She picked up the empty package and began reading the cooking directions as well as the ingredients list. She slowly put the package down and gave me a horrified look.

"Don't worry," I said. "I know they have a little flour-based filler to hold them together, but if you look at the label you'll see there are very few carbs in them."

Without saying anything, she opened the oven and looked at the ribs. She stared at them for a while and then closed the oven door and looked in the refrigerator at what was there. I didn't have any idea what she was looking for, but she was beginning to make me feel uncomfortable.

"Crystal, why don't you go get your salad and dressing? I'm almost ready to start serving."

A few minutes later she returned with a huge bowl of vegetables that had been painstakingly cut into thin strips. There were three different colors of bell peppers, as well as some radishes, cucumbers, carrots, tomatoes, broccoli, cauliflower, celery, and a few alfalfa sprouts sprinkled on top. Although I couldn't see any evidence of it, I suspected there must be some sort of lettuce hiding in there as well.

"That's quite a salad you made there," I said.

"Thanks," she muttered as she removed the cellophane from the top of the bowl and then whisked it along with a bottle of dressing into the other room.

The crab cakes were finished cooking, so I put a serving of one each onto four separate plates.

Crystal returned to the kitchen, "Is there anything I can do to help?"

"You could put the coleslaw and salad dressing, that are in the fridge, on the table if you don't mind."

While she worked on that, I unwrapped four sets of ribs and put one of them onto each of the plates as well. I then called everyone into the kitchen to get whatever plate they wanted. It had always been an unwritten rule in my family that the guests pick first so I waited for either Robert or Crystal to pick a plate. I noticed that Robert was following the 'women first' rule, which in turn meant we all ended up waiting for Crystal to pick a plate. Crystal looked unhappy about the whole concept.

"Take any one you want," Robert urged her.

"Well, I guess I'll take that one," she said, pointing to the closest dish, as the pressure of everyone watching her finally grew strong enough. "But I don't think I'll be able to eat that many ribs. Could you please remove them from the plate?"

"You can just eat as many as you want and leave the rest," I said. "Robert, do you want to take a plate too?"

"I really can't eat that much meat. I'm not really hungry," she said.

"Just take the plate," Robert said to her as he picked out one of the three remaining ones. She looked at him angrily and then took it into the other room without saying a word.

Brad and I took the two remaining ones and followed them into the dining area as well.

The two men chose to sit at either end of the table, which left Crystal and I sitting across from one another. I noticed she took one bite of the crab cake and then moved it and the ribs as close to the outer rim of her dish as she could without having them fall off the edge. She then proceeded to put two large scoopfuls of salad on the remainder of the area. As I watched her pour half of the bottle of dressing that she had brought onto the top of the salad, I noticed it was a low-fat dressing; exactly the opposite of what you would be eating if you were following a low-carb lifestyle. I decided not to say anything about the dressing because I figured she knew what she was doing. After all, it had been Crystal who had taught all of us how to eat low carb to begin with.

"This barbeque sauce is really different and good," Robert said.

"Yes, it's my favorite," Brad said. "Mary Ann has been experimenting with different sauces lately."

"Thank you," I said. "By the way, have we decided what we want to do tomorrow?"

"Not yet," Brad said. "But if everyone decides to hang out here to rest, I'd like to go up to Mendocino and poke around in the shops for a couple of hours. Mary Ann, did you ever firm up your plans with Melissa for the day after tomorrow?"

"No, I haven't talked to her yet, but since I haven't heard otherwise I'm guessing we are still on for me heading down to spend the day with her. Hopefully I'll bring her back to spend the night with us," I said.

"That sounds fine," Robert said. "But after all the driving we did today I'm not up for a big trip tomorrow. Maybe the day after we could go over to Napa Valley and do some wine tasting while you are visiting with Melissa. That is… if everyone else is game."

"I definitely want to do some wine tasting while we are here, but how are you going to feel about missing it Mary Ann?" Brad asked.

"You know me, I'd love to go along, but I'd rather spend time with Melissa," I said. "As long as you guys bring back some good bottles for me to try, I don't have a problem with all of you going without me."

"Crystal, how do you feel about a rest day tomorrow and wine tasting the next?" Brad asked.

"*I* don't really feel like I need to rest tomorrow, but I do want to go wine tasting," she said.

"I'm up for doing something tomorrow afternoon," I said. "But I'm pretty beat from all the traveling today. I would like to sleep in tomorrow and then find some time to walk along the road. I want to get pictures of the ocean and coast-line before we leave. I could always do that in the morning and then, after lunch, we could all go out and do whatever."

"Whatever *you* want," Crystal muttered as she served herself another heaping helping of salad. I couldn't see all of her plate through the flower arrangement on the table, but I was pretty certain she had only eaten a little, if any at all, of the crab or ribs. By this time both Brad and Robert had finished the food on their plates.

"Are you going to eat those ribs?" Robert asked her, pointing toward her dish.

"No, do you want them?"

"Sure… that would be great," he said.

Crystal turned her plate so that the ribs were closest to Robert. As he began to move his dish toward her, she picked the ribs up between her knife and fork and tossed them up in the air, in his general direction. He saw what she was doing and tried to use his plate like a catcher's mitt to intercept them, but he missed and the ribs landed on the teak table, breaking apart upon impact. It was appar-ent from the large pile that resulted, that she hadn't even eaten a bite of them to see what they tasted like. Embarrassed; he picked them up, put them on his plate. Crystal continued to eat her salad as if nothing had happened. I was too stunned to say anything, but after a moment's silence I heard Brad.

"Are there more ribs in the oven?"

"Um, yes… let me help you with that," I said, getting up. He followed me into the kitchen.

"Can you believe she did that?" I whispered to him as I unwrapped another rack of ribs and put it on his plate.

Brad just quietly shook his head back and forth, in apparent disbelief.

I walked back into the dining area and said, "There are also more crab cakes in the kitchen if anyone is interested in them." I could see Crystal was making good progress eating her salad and that her crab cake was still sitting on her plate with only one bite taken out of it.

"I'll have another crab cake in a minute," Robert said.

"Bobby, why don't you just take mine?" Crystal asked.

"You're not planning on eating it?"

"Nope."

"Okay, I'll eat yours when I finish this."

"Whatever."

Both Brad and I sat back down at the table.

"So, tomorrow morning we get to sleep in," Robert said, breaking the silence. "Then we can pick someplace for lunch and talk about what we want to do for the rest of the afternoon, including doing nothing at all. Then, the next day we'll go to Napa while Mary Ann visits with Melissa. We'll need to pick someplace to eat dinner for that night. Perhaps we should talk about that too at lunch tomorrow, after Mary Ann has had a chance to talk to Melissa about her plans."

"Sounds good," I managed to get out. I was beginning to get unhappy about Crystal's behavior. I felt that she was being downright rude. It was clear that Robert was embarrassed by her behavior and trying to divert attention from her. And she didn't even care enough to make it easy for him. When he finished eating her ribs he got up, walked to her, and took the crab cake off her plate.

"Mary Ann, you said there were more crab cakes in the kitchen?" he asked.

"Yes, they are still in the pan on the stove. They have the lid on," I said.

"You don't *have* to eat more crab cakes," I heard Crystal say as he started to walk away.

"I know that I don't have to have them. I *want* to have them. They are very good," he said, giving me a supportive look as he continued toward the kitchen.

"Whatever," she said.

Once he returned, Crystal announced she had promised to call her mother and that she still had her exercises to do this evening. She excused herself from the table, carried her plate into the kitchen where we heard it clatter as though she had tossed it onto the counter. We then heard the back door firmly close as she left the house.

Robert continued to eat his crab as though nothing had happened. Brad and I looked at each other wondering what to say.

"Why don't we get a glass of wine and sit out front on the deck and watch the sun go down," I said.

"Sounds like a plan," Brad said.

"I'll join you both once I finish up here and check in on Crystal," Robert said.

CHAPTER 4

▼

Brad poured three glasses of wine; handed one to me, put one on the table next to Robert and then the two of us went outside. There we grabbed three chairs and pulled them onto the deck in front of the house. The sun was above the ocean, there was still about an hour before the actual sunset would begin.

Before I sat down I noticed that Robert was no longer at the dining room table, but his glass of wine was still there. He must have gone to the guesthouse to check on Crystal without it. I took a large gulp of my wine and then let out a long sigh of relief.

"That was very unpleasant," I said.

"Yes. It was. Very," Brad replied.

"I can't believe how she acted. It was as though she was looking for a fight with all of us all day long," I said.

"Yes, she was… but you didn't have to take her up on the offer," he said.

"What? What are you talking about? What did I do to antagonize her?" I asked. I thought I had been incredibly patient the entire day.

"For one thing, you didn't have to force food onto her plate like that," he said.

"Force food on her plate? I didn't force any food onto her plate. I put servings on four different plates and then I had her take one. If memory serves, that's exactly the way she served her stew the last time we were together. It's also the way food has been served at the dinner parties we've been to in the past couple of months. I don't see what I did wrong," I said.

"Look, you knew she didn't want to eat the ribs and…"

"Yes, that's why I cooked an additional entrée of crab cakes, just so that poor Crystal would have something to eat. Turns out she didn't want that either," I said. I was on a roll now. "Instead she wanted to eat salad with high-carb salad dressing. If she was doing a low-fat diet she could have at least told me so that I could have cooked her something she wanted to eat. She didn't have to make me cook another low-carb thing for her, just so that she could turn her nose up at it. I think her behavior was totally uncalled for and rude and I don't think I have anything at all to be sorry for... especially after having eaten that horrible stew that she cooked for us. I just can't believe you're saying these things to me now."

"What we did was be polite to her, that's all," he said. "Maybe if we had been more understanding and reached out to..."

I understood her plenty.

"That's it," I said. "I don't want to hear anymore about this. I think I've gone beyond the call of duty in this instance. I've been as gracious as any normal person could have been. Maybe it's just that I'm not dazzled by how she looks in a bikini and everything else. Maybe I'm not fooled into thinking that she's perfect just because she always looks perfect." The minute I said it, I knew that I had gone too far and accused him of things he hadn't done. But I really didn't care about his feelings at the moment. I cared about my feelings and I felt he had betrayed me by not understanding how much I had been hurt by what had just happened this evening.

Brad looked at me quietly and finished the last of his wine. Then he put the glass down and said, "I'm going to go for a walk now. I'll be back later. Don't wait up." He then walked down the stairs of the deck to the driveway and headed for the road. I went back to the kitchen and poured myself another glass of wine and by the time I returned to the deck I could barely see him continuing on up the road.

I decided to sit and watch the sun go down, trying to unwind. When Brad and I first got together I used to get so angry when he would leave during a fight. As the years went by I learned that a breathing time during my tirades could be very beneficial for our relationship and I had learned to appreciate Brad's ability to walk away in the heat of the moment. As much as finishing a fight until there was a clear winner would have satisfied me, I was willing to wait until a time when we could talk about it in a more rational manner. I could feel that the wine I was drinking was beginning to smooth some of the rough edges of my feelings. I was feeling much calmer.

I decided to call Melissa and confirm our plans. I got my cell phone and hit the speed dial for her number. Thankfully she was home and agreed that she would be available to meet me for the day and then would probably spend the night. I was glad that soon I would have an ally to give me another perspective about what was going on with everyone here. After I hung up I saw the few clouds above the line of the ocean had begun to take on a more orange color and I knew that sunset was starting in earnest. As I settled back in my chair, I heard the door on the side of the house open.

"Hi, it's just me," Robert said.

"Oh, hi... you're just in time to see the show," I said.

Robert walked onto the deck and I saw that he had his wine glass plus another opened bottle in his hand. He set both of them on the balcony rail and stood looking at the horizon.

"Where's Brad?" he asked.

"He took off for a walk up the road, he'll be back later on," I said.

"I see."

"How is Crystal doing?"

"Fine now. She had a long talk with her mother and seems to be happier. I left her starting her exercises."

I didn't want to seem like I was prying, but after my conversation with Brad I just had to ask, "Was it something I did or said that upset her so much?"

"No, not really. She's just gotten really picky and irrational about her food lately," he said.

"Oh. After watching what she ate this evening I'm beginning to think she must be on a low-fat diet rather than a low-carb one. I just don't understand why she didn't tell us so that I could have made her something she wanted to eat."

"Don't beat yourself up over this. I can't figure out how she's eating from meal to meal myself these days," he said.

I was relieved that he obviously wasn't blaming me for what had transpired this evening. I decided to try to pry some more information out of him.

"What I can't figure out is why she's not eating low carb after all the success she's had doing it. In fact, we've all managed to keep our weight down following her diet guidelines. What's the deal?" I asked.

Before he answered Robert reached for the wine bottle and pulled the cork. He poured himself another glass and then lifted the bottle toward me, asking if I wanted a refill. I nodded in agreement and he topped off my glass as well.

"About a month ago Crystal was turned down for a modeling assignment. She made it into the finals with two other women and after she was rejected she asked why she hadn't been picked. The director told her that although she was a beautiful woman, she was about five pounds heavier than he thought she should be. She's been irrationally obsessed with her weight ever since. Some days she doesn't eat at all, the next she eats nothing but rice cakes and then I'll find her eating nothing but low-carb meals a couple of days later. I haven't figured out what she's thinking, but she gets very upset if anyone tries to give her something that doesn't fit into what she feels like she should be eating at a particular moment. As far as I can tell, she is convinced that she's terribly overweight and feels anyone who can't see that is trying to sabotage her career," he said as he continued to watch the waning light of the sun.

I just had to chuckle. "Crystal thinks she's overweight? She has the most perfect body I've ever seen on any woman alive and she thinks she's fat? If she believes that she must think I look like a moose," I said.

Robert turned around and looked at me puzzled for a minute. Then he said, "Don't ever think like that. You're beautiful just the way you are."

I didn't know what to say or do. I felt myself feeling embarrassed by the personal nature of his comment and I was worried that he could see into my soul, and tell how I really felt about him, as he looked at me. I had expected him to make some sort of moose joke back, not to be so endearingly tender. He must have realized how uncomfortable I was because he continued to talk.

"I apologize for her behavior this evening. She did something quite similar to this, a couple of weeks ago, when we were at one of my associate's house for dinner. She didn't eat hardly anything she was served, and made rude remarks about the meal, but the hostess wasn't as gracious as you were tonight. She started to respond to Crystal's remarks by making comments that were rather harsh about Crystal's behavior. Crystal got very upset and the whole meal turned into a large fight with Crystal taking stabs at how uncouth she found Americans. The hostess started on a jag about why, if the English were so wonderful, did they need to kiss up to the Americans for military and economic protection. I finally had to excuse us and drag her out of there. Every time I've tried to discuss it with her, she has insisted that the hostess was wrong and that she was right. And after her performance here tonight, I'm afraid to take her to anymore business functions until she works these issues out," he said. Then he turned back to watch the sun hovering just over the horizon.

I wanted to get up, walk to him and put my hand over his in a gesture of understanding. But his comment earlier had made me self-conscious and I wasn't sure what he would think of me doing it. I, myself, wondered exactly why I so suddenly had an urge to touch him. Instead I continued to sit where I was and found myself not wanting to even speak.

As the sun hit the horizon line we could actually see it moving, as it appeared to sink into the ocean. Both of us quietly watched this spectacle of nature as the colors became more intensely orange and then slowly turned darker and then finally to black as twilight began. In the old days we would have talked into the night, but it seemed our friendship was growing more distant with the passage of time and all the complications that our relationships with others brought into our lives. Neither of us seemed to want to talk. And with the darkness in front of me and the now blaring lights from the house behind me, I began to feel like I was being displayed on a stage.

"I think I'm going to go inside and wait for Brad to return," I said.

"Yes, I'm going to grab another bottle of wine, if you don't mind, and head back to see how Crystal is doing," he said.

"Why don't you leave the opened one for me?"

"No problem. Although I probably will open mine before I go, just in case there isn't a corkscrew in our kitchenette," he said.

After we finished moving the chairs back to the side of the house, Robert pulled the cork on his bottle and left for the guesthouse. I poured myself the remaining wine in the bottle we had been using and then headed upstairs for bed. I figured Brad would be back shortly, even though he had told me not to wait up. I put the wine glass on the nightstand next to the clock and lay down to rest for a while. I was looking forward to sharing my conversation regarding Crystal's past dinner guest performance with him, but when I closed my eyes I must have fallen asleep because when I woke up and looked at the clock again it was ten-thirty at night. I also noticed that now I had a blanket covering me. It took me a minute to gather my thoughts and realize that Brad had already come to bed. I felt him next to me and could hear the regularity of his breathing. He was definitely fast asleep.

I, on the other hand, felt a little hung over and was now wide-awake. The smell of the wine, on the table beside me, wasn't helping me feel any better; in fact, it was beginning to make me feel queasy. So I got up quietly and tiptoed back to the bathroom and poured the contents of the glass down the sink. Then I pulled the curtains back and peered down at the pool area. I saw the blinds had been pulled closed on the front wall of the guesthouse. Since it appeared all of the lights were off, I guessed that Robert and Crystal had also gone to bed. However, I was wide-awake and I suddenly had an idea for how to get back to sleep. I wanted to go swimming and then sit in the hot tub for a while. I thought that might relax me. I silently returned to the bedroom, got my suit and towel and changed in the bathroom downstairs.

Once I walked outside, the first thing I noticed was that the air had gotten quite chilly over the past couple of hours. It made the water in the pool feel very warm in comparison. I got in and began swimming its length as silently as possible. After I finished a couple of laps I began to feel cold in the water whenever I slowed down a little. The steam I saw lifting off of the hot tub began to look more and more inviting and I decided it was time to get warm. I nearly sprinted the distance between the pool and the Jacuzzi because the air that had felt chilly before was positively frigid now that I had gotten wet. And I didn't want to use my towel because I wanted it dry when I decided I was finished for the evening.

The water in the hot tub felt almost too hot, but once I determined I wasn't going to get scalded from it I quickly sank into its depths and let out a sigh of relief. What initially felt too hot soon turned to being quite comfortable and I found a ledge that served as a seat and perched myself on it. I looked around the edge of the tub and noticed that there were holes for jets and that several feet away there was a timer switch that I guessed controlled them. Quickly I darted over to it and turned it on; setting it for fifteen minutes, hoping it wouldn't make enough noise to wake anyone up. By the time I returned to the tub the jets had started and they were only moderately noisy. I hoped that no one would hear them.

I sank back into the hot water and this time I sat down and rested my head on the edge of the lip around the tub. It was quite comfortable and I watched the wisps of clouds that the wind was moving over the field of stars above me. The moon was still pretty full so I could clearly see, from its light, my surroundings. As the water continued to warm me I relaxed, closed my eyes, and began to reflect upon what had happened during the day.

Even after both of my conversations with Brad and Robert I still felt that Crystal hadn't behaved properly during the day, especially at dinner, but I also felt I could have been more understanding of her problems. Although I was unhappy with my attitude concerning her, I didn't want to be too hard on myself because I reasoned I too had extenuating circumstances. I was exhausted from traveling and from the stress of being someplace new. It was also difficult to be around Robert. As much as I enjoyed his company I always had to make sure I was acting like a good friend and not letting my impulses take over. I could just imagine the look on his face if I had actually put my hand over his when we were on the deck this evening; or, for that matter, the look on Brad's face if he too had witnessed such a thing. It would have felt quite natural for me to have comforted him when it was obvious that he was in psychological pain over what was going on with Crystal right now, but such tenderness on my part could easily be mis-construed by others as something else. And if I searched deep in my heart it was quite possible that indeed it really was something else. As much as I tried to believe that Robert was only my friend, the longings I had for him years ago were still there, only marginally hidden away from my consciousness. It was altogether possible that I would be critical of anything Crystal did because of how I felt about him, but I was fairly certain that in this instance I had been wronged by her treatment of me. I was certain that I would have a better idea of how I was behaving when I saw how Brad reacted to the information Robert had given me about Crystal. Having somewhat found a resolution for my mental dilemma, I concentrated on the way that the water felt swirling around my body in the pool. I was reminding myself not to fall asleep when I heard a click signaling that the timer was turning the jets off.

I was too relaxed to instantly jump up and restart the jets so I stayed where I was, trying to decide what to do next. Except for the faint sound of the ocean waves breaking against the shore it was exceedingly quiet, until I heard something that sounded like a thwack. At first I thought it must be the sound of the wind moving the branches of a tree so that they hit each other. Then I remembered that there weren't any trees within earshot of where I was. I opened my eyes and looked around to see if perhaps there was something hanging on the fence that could make such a sound if the wind moved it. Then I heard it again and realized it was coming from the general direction of the guesthouse and that it sounded more like the palm of a hand hitting flesh, a slap. I could make out in the moonlight that one of the guesthouse windows was open and my heart sank as the thought went through my mind that perhaps Robert and Crystal were having a fight.

I sat up in the tub and tried to be as quiet as possible, listening, to better hear what was going on in the guesthouse and hoping that my first impression of what the sound was and where it was coming from was wrong. In all the years we had been together I had never seen Robert get in any sort of argument with any of his girlfriends. But I recalled the bottle of wine he had taken with him and his quiet and possibly brooding mood earlier in the evening. After what seemed like an eternity, but was really only a few seconds, I heard the sound again and was certain it was the sound of flesh hitting flesh. I grabbed my towel and wrapped it around me as I got out of the tub. I walked as quietly as I could to get closer to the open window, in order to hear better what was going on. After a couple of steps I stopped cold. I could now hear other sounds being made. There was moaning and groaning; I wondered if someone was hurt. Then I heard Crystal's voice.

"Bobby, please don't stop."

Then the moaning got louder and I realized exactly what was happening. I stepped abruptly back and felt a rush of blood to my face as I experienced extreme embarrassment. I knew I was hearing Robert and Crystal having sex and even though it was accidental, I was mortified by my snooping. Time seemed to go into slow motion and I felt as though I was hanging endlessly in this moment. I could still hear them, but I felt like I was paralyzed, unable to move away. Questions were running through my mind. Who had been hitting whom? Had they worked out their earlier problems? But most of all I was curious about the one thing that I had pondered over the years. What was sex with Robert like? As I stood there unable to move, I heard their noises get louder and then they came to an end. I knew then that they had finished what they were doing and when I heard some whispering and then Crystal's muffled giggle it was as though the paralysis evaporated and I was able to move once again.

I scurried across the concrete, back to the kitchen in the main house. Once I was sure I had gotten inside without being discovered, I stopped and caught my breath. I realized I was freezing from the cold night air and began to dry myself off, still trying to comprehend what I had just overheard. I changed out of my suit and back into the pajamas that I had left in the downstairs' bathroom. Slowly I found my body warming up, but I felt my sinuses becoming congested. I suspected that the abrupt temperature changes or the wine I had drank were causing the congestion and I was also concerned I would have trouble sleeping if I laid in bed pondering what I had heard all night. I reached into my purse, which was on the kitchen counter, and pulled out my prescription for an anti-histamine, Zyrtec, figuring it would clear up my sinuses as well as help me to fall asleep.

I quietly crept back upstairs and got into bed without waking Brad. As I lay there, I wondered about Robert. I felt I should feel differently about him given what I had just overheard, but my loyalty seemed to be unwavering. He had always been something of a mystery to me and this only added to his mystique as well as my determination to get to know him better. As I thought about it I could feel the pill taking effect and it wasn't long until I was drifting off to sleep.

When I opened my eyes the next morning the first thing I saw was the digital clock that read nine-thirty. Once I got my bearings, I realized that the medication I had taken the night before, combined with the darkness that the now overcast sky provided, had let me sleep way past a time that I would normally think was reasonable. I turned over and saw that Brad had already gotten up and dressed, leaving his pajamas on top of the bed. I threw the covers off and grabbed my robe and then headed downstairs. I didn't see Brad anywhere, but when I got to the kitchen I smelled the brewed coffee and then saw the note, with a coffee cup on top of it, sitting next to the carafe. It read:

> I've gone to Mendocino for the morning in Robert's car. Have fun taking pictures. I'll be back in time for lunch. Brad.

I poured myself a cup of the coffee and then headed back upstairs. I wanted to shower and get dressed so I could get some photos taken before Brad returned. I was glad he had left me the car because it looked pretty cold outside with the clouds obscuring the sun. After how cold I got last night I decided that I would drive up and down the coastline and get out when I found something worth photographing instead of walking along the road. I showered and found the fisherman sweater I had remembered to pack. This was exactly the sort of dreary day I had brought it along for. I put the sweater on and a pair of comfortable jeans as well as my walking sneakers. I felt functional, yet attractive, as I followed my morning routine of minimal female maintenance. When I was done I headed back downstairs with my camera in tow. I wanted to drink one more cup of coffee before I started off on my adventure.

As I was pouring myself a refill I heard some voices coming from the pool area. I put the carafe down and walked toward the back door, which stood ajar, protected only by the screen door. Now I could clearly hear what was being said.

"I can't bloody believe that you gave him our car!" Crystal said.

"You said that you wanted to stay here and sun next to the pool when I asked you last night," Robert responded.

"It's cold. It's freezing out here. Didn't you notice that before you handed over the keys?" she asked.

"No, it was early and I… when he asked I just remembered what you said you wanted to do," he said.

"Some holiday we're having here. It's like being stranded in an igloo in the middle of the bleeding artic tundra here. I can't bloody believe that you dragged me up here to hang out with these boring, dull people that are your friends. I gave up an audition and a chamber benefit dinner for this. And now you've given away the keys so I can't even get away from all of you," she said.

"It's only for a couple of hours. Mary Ann and Brad will only be gone for a little while longer and then we can go to lunch and go do something else," he said.

"Huh? And I suppose that we'll have to go do whatever she wants to do this time? We all have to walk on eggs around here to make her happy. We all have to worry if she's going to like the house or not, whether she thinks that we liked her cooking or not. Both of you are always worried about what she thinks about everything!" she said.

"If you remember I gave you the option not to come along on this trip. You could have gone to the audition and..." he started.

"Are you mad?" she said. "If you think that I'm going to let you go off for a week and spend time alone with her you're dodgy! I can't believe that you're..."

"Stop! Right now," he said. "Let's go someplace else to discuss this. Now!"

"Sod off!" she said.

"I'm serious," he said more sternly than I had ever heard him speak before.

As I stood there I could hear what sounded like a metal latch being opened. Then I heard the sound of the fence gate swinging shut. I turned my head toward the door leading out to the driveway and saw Robert and Crystal's shadows as they passed by, heading for the road. I hurried upstairs to get a better view of what they were doing and saw that when they got to the road they headed north. Both of them were walking briskly and not talking to each other. I stood, transfixed, watching them go up the road with the wind blowing against them. It seemed that the weather suited their moods.

I suddenly decided that I would try to follow them, if I could manage to do it without their knowing. I grabbed my coat and a long silk scarf that was white with blue flowers. I decided I would wrap it around my hair. It would keep the wind from blowing my hair into knots and might also serve to hide my identity as long as I didn't get too close to them. I also took my camera so I could claim that I was innocently taking the pictures I had talked about last night, in case they spotted me. I went back downstairs and watched them walk up the road until finally they started to veer off to their left, where I could almost make out what looked like a parking lot.

I went out and got into the car. It didn't take long for me to drive up the road and find the cutout that was serving as a parking lot. Since it was a cold day it seemed there weren't many people interested in going to the beach and although I saw one other car, I didn't see anyone but Robert and Crystal when I looked down into the cove. At the top the rim of the cove where I was standing I could see two signs. One of them read 'Observation Platform' and the other read 'Beach,' just as Robert had described the other night at dinner. From what I could see it appeared that Robert and Crystal were headed for the beach on the new trail. I didn't want to follow down behind them so I decided to take the Observation Platform trail. I was finding it difficult to see exactly where the paths were in the side of the cliffs, but I was hoping to be able to get close enough to hear what they were saying without them being able to see who I was. I put the camera strap over my neck, letting the camera hang, and began my journey to the deck. I could see Robert and Crystal still walking along toward the beach.

As I went along I kept an eye on what they were doing. They continued until they got about half way down the cliff, where there appeared to be some sort of space that made a landing. At that point, they stopped and faced each other and began talking. I continued along my path, as it appeared it was taking me closer and closer to them. After about fifty more yards I came to a fork, one was labeled 'Platform Trail' and the other was marked as 'Beach Trail.' I remembered what Robert had said about the old beach path being eroded, but to me it looked in just as good of shape as the observation deck trail did. And following the beach path would definitely take me closer to where Robert and Crystal were. At this point I could almost hear their voices and being a little bit closer might make it so that I could understand what they were saying. I decided to follow the path as long as it appeared to be in good shape, promising myself to stop if it looked in any way degraded.

As I made my way down the path I could hear Crystal's voice getting louder. She also appeared to be getting upset again as her movements were more dramatic. I couldn't hear Robert's voice as well as I could hers, but I could tell he was talking too. I walked yet another fifty or so yards and saw that the width of my path seemed to be getting smaller. In an attempt to be cautious I decided to stop and not follow it any further. I could now hear both Robert and Crystal fairly loudly, but couldn't make out exactly what they were saying. I felt rather frustrated at this point, I couldn't continue safely on and I was so close to being able to hear them. Then I had an idea. I thought that maybe if I looked through the telephoto lens on my camera I would be able to see their faces. And maybe if I could see them, it would help me make out what they were saying. I grabbed the camera and began to look through it. After a couple of seconds I was able to adjust the lens so that both Robert and Crystal were in focus.

"Why don't you just leave me?" Crystal asked. "It hardly feels like you're with me even when you're around."

"I think you're being a little dramatic, don't you?" he replied. "I'm here right now. Willing to spend today doing whatever you want. I even came here so we could…"

At that moment I heard a small sound that I didn't recognize. Then I felt my feet begin to move even though I hadn't taken a step. Everything suddenly went into slow motion as I realized that the ground beneath my feet had begun to move. I tried to move my feet back, looking for firm ground and to get away from the rocks deteriorating beneath my feet. After a couple of steps I felt that I had successfully found solid ground, but then I realized that I had now lost my balance. Realizing I couldn't keep myself from falling I held my camera up with one hand and tried to reach for the ground with my other arm to soften my fall. I never felt my arm hit the ground because the next thing that happened was that I felt a sharp pain on the back of my head. Just as I realized I had hit my head on something, I felt myself slipping into dark blackness, which eventually surrounded me.

CHAPTER 5

▼

Everything was dark. I felt as though I was falling asleep and then suddenly I heard a faint voice.

"Mommy... Mommy... It's time to wake up!" the voice said, getting louder and more insistent.

I fought to open my eyes and when I did I made out the form of a small girl standing, looking down at me.

"She's awake now!" the little girl yelled to someone else, who I could not see in the room. The sound of her voice made me very aware that I had one throbbing headache and I groaned and closed my eyes again.

"She's going back to sleep!" I heard her say, ratting me out to whoever it was that wanted me to get up.

"Use the button to open the curtains. Do you remember where it is and how to use it?" I heard a male voice yell from some distance away.

"Yes, Daddy. I can do it," she said as I heard her move away from me, crossing the room. Suddenly there was a motorized sound and I opened my eyes in time to see a wall of purple velvet curtains begin to open as though they were revealing a screen at a movie theater. Unfortunately they were really opening to let in the light from an incredibly sunny day and I felt my head stab in pain as the bright light hit my eyes.

"I have a headache," I managed to mutter as I pulled the covers, that I felt on my body, over my head.

"She says that she has a headache," my informant yelled to her accomplice.

"Tell her I'll be up in a minute and will get her some aspirin," I heard from the distance.

"Daddy will get you some aspirin," she announced as I heard her leaving the room.

Once I was alone I slowly removed the covers from over my head, sat up, and after I adjusted to the surrounding brightness I saw that I was in an extremely large bedroom with one wall completely compromised of glass. And when I looked out I could see the entire city of San Francisco below me, complete with the San Francisco Bay and the Bay Bridge leading over to Oakland and Berkeley. I decided that I must be near the top of one of the larger hills in the city. Now I knew where I was, but I didn't know why I was here and it didn't explain the little girl who believed I was her mommy.

As I was pondering the answer to these questions I suddenly saw Robert enter the room. He was wearing pants that looked like they were part of an expensive suit as well as a white work shirt, unbuttoned. "Lydia says you have a headache," he said, heading for the bathroom that I could see from my vantage point.

I was so surprised to see him that I instinctively clutched the covers to my chest. Then I realized that I had a complete set of lilac colored silk pajamas on. "Yes, I do," I managed to reply as I loosened my grip on the lavender colored sheets.

I heard him rummaging around in the bathroom and then he returned with two white pills and a glass of water.

"Here you go," he said, handing both of them to me. I took the pills from him and gratefully swallowed them down with the water. "I suppose this means you can't take Lydia to school this morning either," he said.

"Uh, no... I guess that I can't," I said.

"I've got an incredibly busy schedule today, but I'll drop her off on my way in," he said as he went into the closet, got a necktie and then headed for the bathroom.

Curiosity getting the better of me, I climbed out of bed and headed for the bathroom. Although I felt like an outsider I noticed that my pajamas matched the décor of the room exactly. They, if not me, certainly were a part of this environment. Once I reached the bathroom door I could see Robert was tying his tie by watching himself in the mirror. I also noticed my reflection and I was surprised to see that my hair was about four inches longer, with many blonde highlights. Satisfied with the knot he'd just made he turned and briskly passed by me in the doorway, leaving the bathroom.

"When will you get home tonight?" I asked.

"Hopefully at the usual time," he replied quite sharply.

"Why are you angry with me?" I asked.

He turned toward me and said, "You know that you've been looking for a fight with me."

"No," I said. "Really, I'm not looking to fight with you. I swear."

"Fine. I'll be home tonight *hopefully* at the usual time. And, remember your promise to Melissa about not spending too much time talking to her," he said.

"Melissa?" I asked.

"Yes. Melissa. Your friend. The one who has a studio here on the first floor," he said. Then he looked at me quizzically, "Are you sure you're all right?"

"Uh, yes… I'm just not feeling too good with this headache and all. Think I'll go back to bed. Thanks," I said, heading back to the bedroom.

"Do you want me to call you today?" he asked, genuinely looking concerned.

"You don't have to if you're busy. I'm going to rest and I don't know what else I'm going to do," I said. That was honest enough. I had absolutely no idea what I was going to do today.

"Okay, I'll try to," he said as he leaned over to give me a kiss on the cheek. Then he moved and whispered in my ear, "Try to get rid of that headache of yours. I'm feeling like I'm going to have to have some of my needs met tonight." As he backed away from me I could see that he had a smile on his face. I must have had a somewhat shocked look on my face because when he saw it he grinned at me and winked.

"Lydia, it's time to go. Get ready," he said to the little girl who had just entered the room.

"Okay Daddy, I just want to give Mommy a kiss good bye first," she said as she moved toward me. After she delivered a sloppy wet kiss on my cheek she said, "Feel better Mommy," and then headed off after Robert.

I could hear them as they moved about the house and then the noise stopped so I knew that I was alone. Now that it was quiet I had a moment to think about what was going on here. I sort of felt like I was in a dream but everything seemed to be so real that it didn't seem a real possibility that I was actually asleep. Then I remembered what I had read about lucid dreaming; that if you consciously looked at your hands while in a dream they would begin to glow and then you could control what happened next. I figured I had nothing to lose so I held both of my hands out in front of me and gazed at them. No glowing, nothing. So the possibility of this unusual situation being that of a dream was pretty much ruled out. And I didn't seem to have control over what was happening to me either; otherwise, I'd just order the pounding at the base of my head to vanish. It appeared that wherever I was, I was stuck here and I basically had two choices. One would be to lie here in bed with the covers over my head. The other was to get up and try to figure out what was going on. As luck would have it, my head was beginning to feel a little bit better so I opted for the second choice. I found that I was also getting curious about what my surroundings were like. So far I wasn't terribly fond of the décor in the bedroom, but I did like the view. I followed the path that Robert and Lydia had taken and found once I walked through the door that there were two sets of staircases, one leading up and the other leading down. I decided to try going up first.

When I got to the top I found that the same-sized space, that the master bedroom contained, was here divided into four still good-sized rooms. The two rooms that were toward the view of the city also had walls completely made of glass, like the master bedroom had, and they appeared to be a playroom for Lydia and an office that had two desks with computers. The office space, itself, appeared to have been decorated in two distinctly different styles; one more masculine and the other more feminine. The two walls adjacent to the glass walls were totally comprised of bookcases that were full of books. One side looked like it contained a set of law books while the other, on the feminine side, contained lighter reading material such as fiction as well as some expensive-looking leather bound children's books.

The back half of the space had two rooms that were being used as bedrooms; one obviously a little girl's room, decorated with pink frills, with lots of stuffed animals and dolls. The other appeared to be a more grown-up environment, probably the guest bedroom. In between the two rooms was a bathroom with doors leading into each of the adjoining bedrooms.

I returned to the staircase and headed down two flights, noticing that there was yet another set of stairs leading down. There I was greeted by a large room with another wall of glass on the side facing the city. I decided then that the entire side of this building must be made of only glass. Here I saw that the same large space had been divided into a kitchen and dining room area which flowed into a living room. There weren't any walls to be seen, different types of flooring and the type of furniture delineated the space. There were a couple of support beams as well that marked where rooms began and ended.

I returned to the stairs and headed down again. There I found a door leading to the outside as well as another door that, when opened, led to an enormous room. This must have been what Robert was talking about when he referred to Melissa's studio. There were canvases everywhere, some of them were painted and some were in various stages of being finished. There was also a section of the space being used as a ceramics studio and I saw a kiln that appeared to be turned on, baking something inside. From where I was, I could see the entire room and it was clear that Melissa wasn't there at the moment.

I returned to the kitchen upstairs because I really wanted to make a cup of coffee for myself. When I entered I saw that all the appliances had a steel chrome high-tech feel to them. This wasn't at all like the country kitchen I had in my apartment. There wasn't the clutter I had at home either; I saw that the counters here were virtually clear of anything other than a couple of well matched appliances, one of which included a very complicated looking coffee maker. I stood in front of the intimating device and wondered where the coffee itself was kept. Guessing, I opened the cabinet directly below it; and eureka, there were the coffee beans and a grinder for them. I noticed that the coffee was the type that I liked to drink, however, it was not decaffeinated. But I desperately wanted some now, feeling that drinking something familiar would comfort me. So I ground up some beans and figured out how to put them into the filter and turned on the machine. I could hear the bubbling and spitting noises of water and knew that I was only moments away from a nice hot cup of coffee. I then needed a mug to drink from so I opened the cabinet above the maker and found two shelves of coffee cups. I always had been a mug collector and I noticed several of the ones that I had back in college were indeed in this cupboard. As a matter of fact, one of the ones that I had broken last year was sitting there, intact, on the shelf and I smiled when I saw it. I ended up grabbing one that was on the bottom shelf closest to me because it was very attractive and exactly the right size and shape that I liked. I reached down and got some artificial sweetener packets that were in bowl next to the coffee grinder and tore them open, dumping them into the mug. The coffee was finished, so I poured it into the mug as well and then sat down on the sofa that faced the window overlooking the city.

As the warmth from the coffee calmed my nerves, I tried to devise a way to understand my life here. I needed to get information from as many sources as possible without anyone catching on to the fact that I didn't remember a thing about my past. I might be able to be honest with Melissa, if she was the same as I remembered, but I was concerned that other people might think that there was something dramatically wrong with a person who believed that they lived an entirely different life up until they woke up one morning. The place where I thought that I might be able to get the most information without revealing my hand was the office upstairs. I decided that after I finished enjoying my coffee, I would go up and get dressed. Then I would head for any records I could locate in the desks or filing cabinets.

The coffee did make me feel calmer as I drank it and I was engrossed in watching the city below me come alive. I could see the freeways filling up with cars as people tried to get to their jobs downtown. I could even see some people walking on the sidewalks if I looked closely enough. Strangely, it made me feel somewhat lonely to see everyone living their lives out in front of me, while I sat alone on my couch with apparently no place to go. Once I reached the bottom of the mug I put it in the dishwasher, another intimidatingly-modern device, and headed upstairs for the bathroom.

It didn't take long to locate the shampoo and conditioner, as they were already inside the shower stall. They weren't a brand that I was used to, but I used them and they seemed to work just fine. Once I was done showering I found a toothbrush on the side of the bathroom that had female toiletry articles so I brushed my teeth as well. When I went to put the toothbrush back I saw a small dish with some jewelry in it. As I looked at it I realized that one of the rings was a wedding ring, with a square-cut diamond engagement ring soldered to an eternity band made of baguettes. This was very different from the plain gold band that Brad had given me, but it was pretty and I decided I wanted to put it on. Once I slipped it onto my finger, I realized that as much as I wanted to get back home, I also had an overwhelming curiosity about what being Robert's wife would be like. It seemed that now I had a chance to see precisely how things could have turned out. And the first step to take was to do the things that Robert's wife would do. I didn't want anyone thinking that I was acting strange because of small things I had control over. They would probably think I was acting oddly enough as I tried to figure out what they expected of me. I then decided to just put all of the jewelry in the dish on because I wanted to continue with my exploring. There was another ring, which fit on my right-hand ring finger, a pair of earrings, a bracelet and a watch. However, I still needed to get dressed.

The walk-in closet was enormous, with everything neatly hung and stored in compartments. Clothes were separated into three general motifs as far as I could tell; casual things, clothes that looked like business wear and then very formal gowns. Robert's side of the closet was also divided into these categories as well. The clothes were hung on either side with boxy compartments above that held folded sweaters and some books. The back wall had shoe-sized boxes and each compartment neatly stored a pair of shoes. I decided that I wanted to wear casual clothing so I picked a pair of jeans and a colorful tank top with a matching cardigan tied over my shoulders, in case it got cold. A quick search located a pair of Birkenstocks that would work well with the outfit and I slid them on as well. Not surprisingly, they fit my feet perfectly.

Then I headed off on my next mission, to see what I could find out in the office upstairs. I immediately decided to search the desk on the more feminine side of the room. Looking at the top of it I saw a monthly reminder calendar with appointments scribbled for each day. It appeared that I still continued a habit of mine, which was to cross off each day at the end of the day. So I assumed that the first day that hadn't been crossed off was today. Interestingly, the date was the same as it was when I was out walking on the cliffs; and a quick glance to the top of the calendar revealed that even the year was the same. It seemed that I only had one appointment scheduled for today, getting my nails done. I glanced at my nails and laughed. I had never had a manicure before and these nails looked better than they ever had before in my life. I could easily skip getting them taken care of today. I made a note of the name of the salon and then opened the Rolodex on the desk. Once I located the phone number, I called and canceled the appointment. Now my day was free, no one was expecting me anywhere and I could do whatever I pleased.

Further inspection of the calendar revealed that apparently I didn't have a steady job, instead I spent my time attending luncheons, organizing various events, was very active in the PTA and I spent a great deal of time having myself pampered at various salons and spas around town. At least this explained the variety of clothes I'd found downstairs in the closet. As I was opening the drawers of the desk, looking for files that might contain personal documents, I heard a sound. It seemed that someone was climbing up the stairs.

"Hola," the female voice yelled.

"Hello?" I said.

Suddenly an older, Hispanic-looking woman peeked her head through the door and said, "Hola, missus Mary Ann."

"Hi," I said.

She pointed to the waste paper can next to my desk, "Garbage?"

Not knowing what to do, I agreed, "Garbage, yes."

She entered the room carrying a big plastic garbage bag and emptied both of the waste paper cans into it. Then she left the office and I heard her go into the other rooms briefly and then back downstairs. I suspected that she must be the cleaning woman and again I just laughed. This house looked remarkably clean and I wondered how often she came and how long she would be here cleaning today.

Once I was certain that I was alone again I continued searching the contents of the desk. I found an odd assortment of things, but nothing that looked like official files. So I went to the other desk and began to inspect it. This desk was impeccably neat and orderly. There was a picture of Robert, Lydia and myself on top of it that seemed to have been professionally taken, not very long ago. Other than that, there was an expensive looking clock and a black statue of a cowboy riding a broncing horse. When I looked in the middle desk drawer it was more out of curiosity than a search for papers. As I suspected, the drawer was a very neatly organized collection of pens, paperclips and rubber bands. It reminded me of the closet in the master bedroom. I then began opening the side drawers and on the second try I hit pay dirt. This entire drawer was full of hanging file folders, each carefully labeled. I found very fat folders labeled things like Loans, Mortgages, Renovations, Refinance and at the very back in a slim little file I found the label Personal. I pulled it out and found four pieces of paper in it. Two of them were Robert and my birth certificates. The other, more interesting, documents were Lydia's birth certificate and a wedding certificate that said Robert and I were indeed married.

The marriage certificate indicated that Robert and I had gotten married at about the same time that Brad and I were married, but that Robert and I had gone to Las Vegas, Nevada to take our vows. Brad and I had gotten married on the East Coast. It was strange, but even as I sat there holding a paper that said that I was legally Robert's wife, I still felt that I was married to Brad and that just by reading this paper I was somehow cheating on my husband. But this document clearly stated that for the past seven years I had been Mary Ann Monroe, not Mary Ann Radcliffe.

I then turned my attention to the last piece of paper, the birth certificate for Lydia. I read my name on the line for the mother and as I suspected, I saw that Robert had been designated as her father. So Lydia was our child together. I wasn't terribly surprised because as I looked at her in the picture on the desk in front of me I could see both Robert and myself in her. She had his eyes and impish smile while her hair coloring and the shape of her face was more like mine. If I had to say who she looked more like I would have said myself, but that may have been because I knew what I looked like as a child and I'd never been privileged enough to see photos of Robert when he was young.

I then looked at the birth date so that I'd know exactly how old she was. The date indicated that she was now six years old, so we must have had her right after we got married. Curious as to when she was conceived I counted back nine months from her birthday and then compared that to our wedding date. To my surprise I found that Lydia appeared to have been conceived two months before we got married, unless she was a premature birth. I wondered how all of this had come about. And then I felt a wave of total panic, I was in way over my head and didn't know what to do next.

Although I had always had fantasies about being with Robert, they were always along the line of holding his hand or kissing him for the first time. I never imagined that I would be dumped into a relationship with him that had been going on for at least seven years, much less without any knowledge of what had transpired. We had a history together and I had no idea of what it was. I didn't even know how my own child had come to be conceived and why she didn't have any other siblings. The more these thoughts ran through my head the more panicked I became. And the more my headache made itself apparent that it hadn't left.

I sat back in the leather chair that I noticed for the first time was very comfortable. I closed my eyes and tried to calm myself by regulating my breathing. I tried to convince myself that this really was a dream, that nothing I did here would really influence my life as I knew it. I tried to believe I was back home and that when I opened my eyes I would be back with Brad, either on the Northern California coast or back in our apartment outside of Boston. I hoped that if I believed it enough it would be true and then I slowly opened my eyes. What I saw before me was the glass wall in a building overlooking the city of San Francisco. For whatever reason, I was here and I couldn't figure out a way to get home.

I sat back in the chair and let out a sigh. Perhaps I was here for a reason, maybe there was something that I needed to learn or perhaps I needed to do something in order to return home. In any case, I only had a matter of hours before Robert was going to come back and I needed as many questions answered as I could get in order to be able to deal with him. I started to leaf through the other folders to see if I could find out what kind of debt load we had or anything thing else that I could find of interest.

As I was pulling out one of the folders I heard a female voice, "Lover? You up there?"

"Melissa? Is that you?"

"Yes, it's me," she said. "You going to keep me company or what?"

"I'll be right there," I said, returning the files to their original location. Numbers could wait until later.

CHAPTER 6

▼

As I hurried down the stairs, I had a smile on my face. Things here might be very different from what I was used to, but it appeared that Melissa was still my friend and that at least parts of our early years together were the same as I remembered. I knew this because she had referred to me as lover. Back when we were in high school some of our male friends had teased us, saying that we were closet lesbians because we spent so much time together. We had laughed at their immaturity over thinking, much less saying, such a thing and then Melissa had taken to calling me 'lover' as a joke. Since she called me that this morning I could assume my life up until that moment, at least, was the same as I remembered it. Hopefully she would be able to enlighten me as to where the shift in events occurred. But even if she couldn't, I was happy to see her again.

I peeked into the floor with the living room on my way down to the studio and found both Melissa and the cleaning lady there. Melissa was in the kitchen pouring herself a cup of coffee and I decided I wanted another one as well.

"Thanks for making me some java," she said.

"No problem. I needed some pretty badly myself this morning. And now I need some more," I said.

"Beautiful day today. Too bad I was out late last night. I'm a little hung over and don't feel much like working," she said.

I poured my coffee and then watched her add a very large splash of milk to her cup.

"Dessert coffee," she murmured, scooping a large spoonful of sugar as well.

I smiled. Dessert coffee was another tradition that dated back to our high school days.

When she was done I followed her down the stairs and found a place to sit as she stood in front of the glass wall looking down upon the city. She still wore her dark brown hair long, down to her waist and she still dressed her petite figure in a colorful, artistic way. I never knew what she would be wearing each time I saw her because it seemed that she considered her body a canvas and was always experimenting on how to paint it in a new and interesting manner. Today she reminded me of a Picasso, bright colors put together in a visually stimulating way.

"Robert told me that I'm not supposed to bother you very much today," I said.

"Robert worries too much," she said, turning around to face me. She then walked over to a comfortable looking couch, sat down on it and pulled her legs up in what looked like a yoga position. She continued to drink her coffee as she looked at me, "You look different today Marilyn."

I must have looked as confused as I felt because she quickly added with a slight giggle, "Oh, I'm sorry. You're not dressed like Marilyn Monroe today, are you? What, no high society teas?"

It still took me a minute to figure out that she was making a joke about my name; she obviously was teasing me that I was Marilyn Monroe instead of Mary Ann Monroe. "No, I'm just plain old Mary Ann today," I said.

"No. You're not plain Mary Ann today either," she said, getting up and beginning to walk around me. "There's something decidedly different about you today lover."

I was beginning to feel uncomfortable as she stared at me from different angles. Finally she stopped in front of me and said, "Why don't you let me sketch you. You can talk to me and tell me all about it."

"I don't know if I could stay still enough for you today. I woke up with this awful headache," I said, hoping that would be excuse enough to get me off the hook for being a model.

"I'll let you take breaks whenever you want. I'll even let you have one of my clovies if you sit for me," she said as she dug a pack of clove cigarettes out of her tote bag. She handed one to me and then put one in her mouth and lit it. It had been literally years since I'd had one of these, but I decided to have one with her and sit for her as well. I allowed her to light my cigarette after she finished lighting hers; officially striking the deal between us.

"Since you're wearing jeans… Can I assume that you don't have any appointments today?" she asked as she dug a large sketchbook out of a pile of papers sitting in one of the corners.

"I did have one, but I called and canceled it. It was for getting my nails done," I said.

"Bad news. Frederick is going to show up here anyway to do your nails. Cynthia says that he never checks his messages in the morning. Good thing too. If you skipped your first appointment with him he'd never let you set up another," she said. "What time were you expecting him?"

"Not until four," I said.

"Great. We have until three then. When Lydia gets home from school," she said. "I should be able to finish." She sat back down on the couch facing me, sketchbook on her lap, smoke rising from the cigarette, resting in an ashtray, on the table beside her.

For a while we enjoyed smoking in silence, the only sound being the scratching of Melissa's charcoal on the previously blank page of the sketchbook. I was surprised that I wasn't choking and hacking from the clove smoke as I inhaled even more deeply. This body appeared to be used to an occasional cigarette whereas I knew my previous one wouldn't accommodate to this behavior as easily. As I set my cigarette down into the ashtray next to me I watched Melissa carefully. She was quite intent as she looked at me briefly and then concentrated on translating what she saw to the page in front of her. Even though she said that she noticed a change in me, I had to admit that she appeared exactly the way that I remembered her and I was beginning to feel quite at ease in her presence.

The longer I sat still, the more my mind became active. I began to muse about how Melissa would react if I told her the truth; that I apparently remembered nothing of my life between high school and this morning. I knew that she held the answers to many of my questions, because I sensed that our relationship was the same as it had been before. I always told her my secrets in the past; I guessed that I would have done the same here.

As I reflected on my dilemma, I finally came to the conclusion that the Melissa I knew would have kept my secret and tried to help me if I asked her to. At least for a while she would have, until it appeared that the secret was harming me in some way. A careful presentation of my situation to her would possibly yield the results that I was looking for; answers without too many worries on her part. But I wondered how to start a conversion about this. I took one long last puff on the cigarette and then extinguished it by pressing the burning tip into the ashtray.

"Did you know that you're scowling and that you have those little worry wrinkles on your forehead?" she asked.

"No, I'm just thinking about something."

"Want to tell me what's bugging you now?" she asked, leaning forward, offering me yet another cigarette. "You and Robert have a fight or something?"

"No fight," I said as I leaned toward her, accepting her offer. This time I just held the cigarette in my hand as comfort.

Melissa again turned her attention to sketching, but I knew that she was expecting me to talk about my problem. I decided that I really had nothing to lose by telling her what I believed and that I potentially could gain a lot of information.

"Look," I began hesitatingly, "I really would like to tell you what's bothering me, but I know that what I'm going to say is going to sound pretty wacky. If someone told me this I would think that they needed to be locked up in a loony bin. If I tell you, I need for you to have an open mind and to, at the very least, promise me that you won't tell anyone else."

She stopped sketching and looked at me intently, "I'm intrigued. Continue. Your secrets are always safe with me."

"Okay. Here goes," I said, quickly searching for words that might even remotely sound sane, but would describe what I had been experiencing. "I guess the best thing to do is just to say it. However crazy it might sound to you…" I took a deep breath and after releasing it I blurted out, "Up until this morning, when I woke up, I was living a totally different life. I had an apartment on the East Coast, outside of Boston, with Brad as my husband and no child. I was on vacation here, up north, following Robert and his not-so-nice girlfriend while they were arguing and I fell down. Next thing I know Lydia is waking me up." There, I'd told her. It had sounded just as nuts as I had predicted it would, but when I finally got the courage to look up from the cigarette that I was manipulating in my hand to see her face, I felt better. She looked concerned, but also fascinated by what I had just said.

"Well lover, that would explain your new look and attitude. But how do you think that this happened?" she asked.

"I have no idea. At first I thought that this was a dream, but I'm pretty sure that it isn't because it feels way too real at this point," I said. "I don't know how this happened and I don't know how to undo it. It's possible that I need to do something or learn something from being here, but I don't have any idea what it is."

"Since *I* feel just as real today as I did yesterday, I'd have to agree that this isn't a dream," she said. "Do you have any idea of exactly when your life path diverged into this one?"

"Not really. I know that high school must have been the same because you're here and you are the way that I remember you. However, in my old life you have an apartment that you use as a studio as well. It's down in Noe Valley, over a music shop. And looking around here I'd say that your art in my other life is a little more primitive in nature," I said.

"Interesting," she said as she set the sketchbook aside. She leaned forward with the lighter extended in my direction, "I think that you should light that fag."

I laughed, "Okay, but I'm not a smoker."

"Today you are," she said, smiling as I drew in a deep breath through the cigarette. "You mentioned that you married Brad. Doesn't that mean that you must have gone to the same college in your other life? When did you meet Robert and marry Brad?"

"I saw Robert the first week of college, but didn't meet him until much later; he was a friend of Brad's. I met Brad shortly after I spotted Robert and began dating him fairly quickly. We got married right after we graduated and then moved to Boston. Robert went on to law school," I said.

"Ah…" she said, sitting back. "Here, you were engaged to Brad while in college, but you and Robert got together right before graduation. You told me that you and Brad got into a fight about your upcoming wedding and you went to see Robert. The two of you slept together that night and shortly after that you found out that you were pregnant with Lydia. In what must have been a pretty unpleasant scene, you and both Robert and Brad decided that you would marry Robert."

"That was probably a wise decision given that Lydia is Robert's child," I said.

"Interesting that you should say that," she said. "One of the things that the three of you worked out during that infamous meeting was the fact that none of you knew who Lydia's father was. You had slept with both of them during the month that she was conceived. The agreement reached was that you would marry Robert and he would raise Lydia as his own, but that Brad has visitation privileges. One other stipulation, that I've never understood, is that a paternity test would never be done. None of you really wanted to know whose child she is."

"That's an odd arrangement," I said. "Given what I know from the life that I did lead, is that I'm fairly certain that Lydia is Robert's. I even can see some of his features when I look at her, but mostly I think that she looks like me. I wonder if I should say something about it."

"I wouldn't if I were you. But if you decide that you must, you're going to get your chance. Tomorrow is the first Saturday of the month and that's Brad's day to come here and take Lydia out."

Even though I couldn't tell whether she was taking my memory loss seriously or not, I could tell that she was more than willing to talk to me about my life. I decided to keep asking her questions, and to keep going until she seemed bored, tired or suspicious of me.

"Is he married now?" I asked.

"Yes, he got married to Jeannie about a year ago, but she doesn't generally come along for these visitations," she answered.

"Where does he live?"

"Down in Silicon Valley. He moved out here at the same time that you and Robert did. After law school," she said.

"Is he happy?"

"Seems to be. Pretty much I guess," she said. "Of course, I never really got to know him before, when you were going out with him."

"How about Robert and me? Are we happy too? Just asking because this morning when I asked him a question, he sort of barked his reply back at me."

She chuckled. "Well, if being madly in love with a guy could make you happy, then you should be the happiest woman on earth. You decided to marry him because you were insanely in love with him. I can say that I haven't seen any evidence of that having changed over the years. But your relationship with him isn't the 'happily ever after' most of us dream of when we are girls."

"What do you mean?" I asked.

"You don't seem to mind, but he's rather controlling. He likes to have things just the way that he wants them," she said. "Keeping him happy has changed you a little over the years."

"I'll say," I said. "I look around this house and I don't recognize it as being something that I created. Even my clothes aren't the sort of thing that I would identify as being mine, except the casual ones, like what I've got on."

"Good guess on the decorating. You wanted to decorate it yourself, but in the end the two of you couldn't agree on what you wanted. So you hired an interior decorator and mostly just said yes to whatever he suggested. I must say that everything matches quite nicely," she said, giving me a coy smile.

"Speaking of this house. It's quite unusual. How did we come to live here and how did I convince you to keep me company up here?" I asked.

"After Robert graduated from law school he got an offer from a prestigious law firm here in the city. You weren't really keen on living here in Frisco, but tried to keep an open mind. One of your conditions was that you wanted a view if you had to put up with the crowds of people. The two of you went driving and tried to find the highest point that was still within the city. You can't see it from here, but a couple of streets up behind this house are the antennas for several radio, as well as, TV stations. You also can't see from here that there are four buildings identical to this one. This used to be an apartment complex. Anyway, you came up here and copied down the addresses of several of the houses that you liked. Later, after the interview and the generous offer from Robert's law office, he went to the Registry of Deeds and tracked down the owners of the buildings you were interested in. Most of them declined to entertain your offer to buy them out. But the fella that owned these four buildings was having some financial problems so he agreed to sell you one of the end units. The other three are still owned by him and are still apartments today, but mostly only professionals can afford them and they make good neighbors. It took almost a half a year to gut this building and renovate it into a single family home," she said. "Oh yeah, you offered to let me work up here in return for occasionally taking care of Lydia. I honestly thought at the time that you wanted me here so that you wouldn't be so lonely. Robert works long hours most of the time, especially when you first moved here."

"Oh," I said, thinking about what it must have been like waiting for this place to be fixed up so that we could move into it.

"You really don't remember any of this?" she asked.

"I really don't remember any of this at all," I said. "You said that Robert is controlling. What exactly do you mean by that?"

Melissa looked at me for a minute and I sensed that she was a little uncomfortable. "Maybe I'm being overly sensitive and stating it too harshly," she said. "It's not like he demands that you do things. It's just that he always makes it clear when he isn't happy with what's going on and in the end you usually do whatever you can to make him happy. And that's not to say that it's all one way. He did bend over backwards to make you happy by getting you this house. There's just a lot of compromising that goes on around here, but I always sense that you give in more because you are so in love with him. On the other hand, he always gives in to whatever Lydia wants. The sun rises and sets upon that child for him."

"Marriage is compromise," I said.

"And a lot of hard work, according to you, as well," she said.

"So, he really loves Lydia and is a good father. But he's not sure that she's his," I said as I wondered about what that must be like for him.

"Yes. That's true. But Brad loves that little girl as well. He's been trying to get you guys to agree to let him take her east to see his family for an extended period of time. It's been the hot topic of conversation over the past couple of weeks around here. You're supposed to give him your decision when he arrives here tomorrow," she said.

"This must really be a hard situation for everyone. How does Lydia handle it?" I asked.

"Lydia has always had a mommy and a daddy and Brad who comes to visit her at least once a month. To her, this is all normal. But the trip east to see his family might cause her to start questioning the situation. At least that's what you and Robert have been worrying about recently. None of you want to hurt Lydia though. The question is, what's the best for her as well as the three of you," she said. "I'm glad that I don't have to make these decisions. I feel for all three of you. But Lydia is a beautiful child. You've made good choices up to now and I'm guessing that you all will work it out so that she'll continue to be emotionally healthy."

"Sounds easier said, than done," I said.

"Yep," she said as she picked up the sketchbook and began working on it once again. We both sat in silence for a bit and then she paused to get another cigarette and extended the pack toward me, offering me yet another one.

"My headache is getting worse from smoking those. I'll pass," I said.

She stopped sketching long enough to light her cigarette and then she gave me a long look as though she was determining whether she wanted to say something or not. "I'll tell you what. I took a hypnosis class last year and I might be able to get rid of your headache. Do you want me to try?" she asked.

I didn't have to think about it at all, I would have done anything to get rid of the pain. "Yes, please do. What do I have to do?"

"Not much, except relax and try to be open to suggestion," she said. "But, before we start I would like to go over what I'm planning on saying to you so that it's less frightening. Should make it a pleasant experience for you. Is that okay?"

"Yes. Absolutely. I've never been hypnotized before. Sounds like fun."

She got up from the couch and went to the desk, located on the side of the room, and began rummaging through one of the drawers. She appeared to find what she was looking for and headed back to the couch. She motioned for me to join her, so I did.

"After we finish up here, remind me to show you the painting that I finished," she said.

"Okay. No problem."

"Now, this is going to be pretty straightforward. I'm going to have you look at this card," she said as she held up a five by seven piece of paper with a black and white pattern, which spiraled inward, toward the center. "I'll give you some commands, the first of which should induce you into hypnosis. Then I'll make some suggestions, and that will be how I determine if you are hypnotized. Understand so far?" she asked.

"Yes, I'm ready."

"Not so quick. I'm going to give you the suggestion that you will wake up refreshed and feeling well. This should get rid of your headache, as well as make you wake up in your old past if this is all a dream. Does that sound good?" she asked.

"Yes, that's a great idea."

"Is there anything else you can think of that we should try while we are at it?"

"No. And I really appreciate that you believe what I've been telling you."

"Okay, let's start then," she said. "I want you to look at this card and concentrate on it. Look at how the pattern moves toward the middle. Notice how the pattern flows to the center. Now I want you to count backwards from ten. As you count your eyelids will begin to get heavy. When you reach six they will be so heavy that they will close and you will be in a deep sleep. Begin to count now."

I was concentrating on the card, but I felt totally awake. I began to count backwards, "Ten, nine, eight, seven, six." Oddly enough as I counted my eyelids did begin to feel heavier and I was surprised when I reached six and they closed all by themselves.

"Alright," I heard Melissa say. "I have a penny. This penny is very heavy and when I place it on your right hand it will be so heavy that you will not be able to lift your hand at all. When I remove the penny you will be able to lift your hand normally."

I felt her place something small on my hand and then I heard her say, "Okay, the penny is on your hand, try to lift it."

I tried to lift my hand but to my surprise, was unable to do so. "You can stop trying now," she said. Then I felt her remove the penny. "The penny is gone, try to lift your hand now," she said. When I tried to move my hand, this time it lifted up normally.

"Good. Now you can put your hand down. What you are going to do now is begin counting backwards from five. With every number that you count you will become more awake and when you reach one you will be fully awake and feel refreshed and well," she said. "Begin counting now."

"Five, four, three," I said as I began to feel more awake. "Two, one." When I reached 'one' I opened my eyes and found myself in Melissa's studio overlooking the city, but my headache was totally gone. I breathed out a sigh of relief.

"Feel better?" she asked.

"Yes. I can't believe it. Thank you very much," I said. "But I'm still here, not where I should be at all."

Melissa gave me a quizzical look, "Were you really expecting to find yourself someplace else?"

"I think that *hoping* would be the word for it, not *expecting*," I answered. "However, I'm not really sure that I'm ready to go back yet." As the words came out of my mouth I realized that this was true. As uncomfortable as these new surroundings were, there was an air of excitement that had been missing from my life before.

"Why is that?" she asked.

"Well, it's hard to explain, but I've spent over ten years wondering what it would be like to be with Robert and now I have my chance. If I returned to my old life now I'd never get to know what he's like," I said.

"Maybe that's what you need to do then. Before you can go back, I mean," she said.

"Maybe. But it's going to be so hard. And that's putting it mildly. Even though I have a piece of paper upstairs that says that I've been married to Robert for seven years, my heart still feels that Brad is my husband. If I sleep with Robert I'm going to feel like I'm being unfaithful, irregardless of what my intellectual side tells me."

She sat in silence listening to me. I sat across from her, looking out onto the city. "May I have one of those now?" I asked, pointing to the pack of cigarettes.

"Sure. I'll have another clovie as well," she said. As she took one from the box she said, "Oh yeah, I wanted to show you that painting I told you about."

"That sounds good," I said taking a cigarette from the box. As I lit mine, Melissa got up and walked over to the side of the room and started flipping through a set of canvases that were resting against the wall.

"I put it over here where no one could see it. At least until I finished it and showed it to you. It's pretty much exactly what you asked for, except for my artistic interpretation, of course. I hope you like it," she said.

She pulled a large canvas from the pile and turned it around so that I could see it. I involuntarily gasped once it was facing me. It was a painting of the Northern California coastline cliffs, with the ocean on the left side and a giant willow tree on the right. Standing next the tree, sort of in the middle, was a woman who looked very much like I did ten years ago. She was looking toward the ocean with a forlorn look, as though she was thinking about a lost love or waiting for her love to return from the sea. The colors were muted blues, browns and greens for the ocean, ground and tree. But beneath the willow tree, where the woman was standing, was a meadow of purple flowers. There was a little breeze coming in from the ocean because the woman's long brown hair and the willow tree appeared to be effected by it. As I looked at it I almost felt that I could walk into the scene and I felt very deeply affected by it.

"So. How do you like it?" she asked.

"I'm speechless. It's so beautiful. I asked for this?"

"Yes lover," she said. "I wanted to give you something special for your birthday last year and this is what you asked for. Sorry it took me so long, but I wanted to get it right. It's you. Back how you were when we were in high school. When your hair was really long. I tried to capture your longing for something else. You always struck me as wanting to get out of there, to find something new. And I worked in the purple so that it could go in your bedroom, as requested."

"It's the most wonderful gift that anyone has ever given me. It feels so real to me too, as though I could step into it," I admitted.

"Good. I think that's the nicest thank you I've ever gotten. I'm so glad that you like it. I finished it up last night and then went out and had a few too many gin and tonics," she said. "I hope that it passes the 'Robert test' and that he approves of it."

"I don't care what Robert thinks of it. I love it. Let's put it up in the bedroom today. But I'd like to get something to eat first. How about you?" I asked.

"Sure, I'm a little hungry," she said. "But after we finish eating and hanging I'll need to get back to working on this sketch, if you don't mind."

"No problem," I said.

We headed up to the kitchen and I looked through the refrigerator. There wasn't much in there that wasn't low in fat and high in carbs. After some searching around I located some eggs, vegetables and cheese. I decided to make us two omelets. Melissa got herself another cup of coffee, emptying the pot. She asked me if I wanted more and then made another pot when I said that I did. As odd as this situation felt to me, I was comforted by how natural it felt to be around her. After I finished cooking our brunch we sat down at the dining room table and began to eat.

"You're certainly not worried about your weight or your health anymore," she said.

"What do you mean?" I asked.

"This is a far cry from the low-fat rice cakes we usually have here in the morning," she said. "Why, this is a heart-stopping plate of cholesterol," she added with a slight southern drawl.

"I've learned that it's not the fat that causes our bodies problems," I said. "It's really the carbohydrates that we eat. It's complicated and has something to do with insulin production, but trust me, this is much more healthy than rice cakes."

"Robert's going to slip a gear if you try to feed him like this tonight," she said with a giggle.

"Then I guess that I'm going to have to dress it up and make it look more healthy to him. Maybe I can find some fish and exciting vegetables here in the kitchen," I said.

"Don't worry. Today is the day that the groceries come. You should have plenty of veggies and non-red-meat products to work with," she said.

"The groceries are delivered?" I asked.

"Yes. Every Friday. Like clockwork."

"Well, that sure makes things easier."

It didn't take us long to finish eating the omelets and then to fetch the painting and head upstairs. When we got to the bedroom I instantly knew which of the art works hanging on the wall I wanted to replace with my new treasure. Across the room from the bed was another large painting that was abstract in nature and just about the same large size as the one that Melissa had painted for me. It only took us a matter of minutes to take down what was there and replace it with the new one. After we had put it in place I stepped back to the area of the bed and looked at it.

"That's just absolutely perfect. I can't thank you enough. And although I don't know what you've given me as gifts over the past seven years I can say that this is the best gift that I ever remember being given. It's exquisite," I told her.

"Thank you. I'm so very happy that you like it. And I must say that it brought me pleasure to paint it for you," she said. After we stood there looking at the painting for a while she continued, "The only thing that has me worried is what Robert is going to think about you unilaterally replacing it for something that the decorator picked out."

I nodded as I thought about what she had said. "I think that the best solution would be to take this old one upstairs to the office, and if he finds that he can't live without it, he can put it up on one of the walls there. I'll even let him put it on my side if he's that distressed about it," I said.

Melissa looked at me with what I could only describe as approval. Then she got a worried look on her face. "I like you, like this. I really do. But I'm not sure how Robert is going to take to the 'new you.' I'm beginning to really believe that something mystical has happened to you."

"Well, I can't tell you how much I appreciate your faith in me. At first I was afraid to say anything to you, because I thought that you'd think that I'd gone over the edge, into insanity. This all sounds crazy, even to me, let me tell you," I said.

"I'm glad that you told me, but I'm not so sure that you should tell anyone else about this. If you try hard you might be able to act the way that you used to. Then they won't guess," she said.

"I'm going to have trouble if I can't be myself. I'm used to being self-sufficient. I worked at a difficult job and I was very good at it. But, on the other hand, I really am interested in seeing what being with Robert would be like. I was so in love with him once. And if I'm honest with myself, I still love him. So it might be worth toning down my personality if I can be with him in return. Maybe I can just play it cool while trying not to lose myself," I said, attempting to work through my various emotions about this situation.

"If anyone can do it, you can. Especially this new you. I don't think that he'll kick you out of bed for replacing the painting, but it will be out of the ordinary for you to have put it up without consulting him," she said.

"Maybe I'll just feign remembering talking to him about it and getting his permission. I hate doing that, but watching people do business with Brad has taught me maneuvering like this can be a very successful strategy for getting what you want," I said.

Of course, the minute I said it I remembered my marriage with Brad and again felt a pang of guilt over plotting a way to make my relationship with Robert work. But, I reasoned, I was in an odd situation and the old rules did not apply. I needed to be able to function here and as long as I continued to work on finding a way home I felt that my conscience should be clear.

"Whatever you do, just don't let on about what's going on in your head," she said.

"Got it," I said. "I suppose that we should go back down and let you finish up that sketch. The afternoon's starting to get away from us."

"Yes. I do want to finish if I can."

We carried the abstract painting up the flight of stairs and put it in the office, resting against Robert's desk. If he wasn't too attached to it I determined that I'd check and see if it was better or worse than what was in the guest bedroom and maybe make a switch there. I didn't find it objectionable; I just didn't love it the way that I did my new gift. After we got done there we returned back to Melissa's studio and I settled in so that she could continue sketching.

"Want another clovie?" she asked as she helped herself to one.

"Sure. My head feels great now. Thanks," I said as I took another one from the box. "Oops. This is the last one. Maybe I shouldn't have it."

"I have a couple more boxes of them in my purse. Go for it. But I should mention that you're going to need to take a shower and brush your teeth before Robert gets home. He really, really doesn't like it when you smoke," she told me.

"Oh yeah. He wouldn't, would he? His mother died of lung cancer from smoking. I remember him ranting and raving about second-hand smoke when we were in college," I said.

"You got it. And I don't want to be responsible for my lover getting kicked out of her house because I gave her lots and lots of calming clovies," she said with a slight giggle.

"We can't have that, that's for sure. I'll bathe after I get done with the nail guy. You said his name was Frederick?" I asked.

"Yep. And I can't wait until we meet him. Cynthia sure has some stories that she tells about him," she said.

We sat in silence as Melissa continued to sketch. I finished my 'clovie' and then sat still as I gazed out over the city. The sun was burning brightly and I guessed that we were at the hottest point of the day. The people who I saw moving about near us were all wearing shorts and tank tops. I absent-mindedly commented on it to Melissa.

"Yes," she said. "It's hot now. But when the fog comes in, it gets amazingly cold. Especially up here. Since we are at the top of the hill, sometimes it's like I drive into a cloud as I make my way up. Beautiful days like today are glorious, but we do spend a lot of time up here like damp little mushrooms."

"But it must be spectacular at night with the city lights on."

"Yes. But you get to enjoy that more than I do. I'm mostly only here during the day hours. My nights I spend down in the city," she said. Melissa continued to draw for a while and then she stopped and looked at me concerned again. "You know, if your head starts hurting again or if you continue to not remember your past, you might want to consider going and seeing a doctor."

"A doctor? I don't want to go tell someone that my memory of my life up until this point is different than what everyone else believes. They will lock me up for sure," I said.

She gave me a long, thoughtful look and then hesitatingly spoke, "Not necessarily. The headache might indicate that you hurt yourself someway and that could be causing your memory problems. It might be a physical problem; not a psychological problem like you're worried about."

"True. I hadn't considered that. I'll tell you what. If I'm still here, or still having what you are considering memory problems, I'll go see a doctor on Monday. After the weekend is over. And I'll go sooner if my headache comes back. Does that make you feel better?" I asked.

"Yes. Better. But I'm still going to worry about you. Why don't I come up here tomorrow afternoon? After Brad brings Lydia back. That way I can see how you are doing."

"That would be great. I'd really appreciate it. Also, is there someway that I can get a hold of you if things get bad up here? Do I have your phone number?" I asked, trying to think ahead, to what problems might occur.

"In your purse you have a cell phone. My home and cell number are in its memory. Just press the down arrow until you come to them and then hit send. I'll keep my cell turned on all weekend, just in case," she said.

"That would be great. Hopefully I won't need you, but you never know," I said. I watched as she turned her concentration back to her drawing. My promises had seemed to calm her worries and I could tell that she was beginning to relax a bit.

"Just a few more minutes and I'll be finished with this. I don't want to show it to you until I transfer it to canvas and paint it. You know how I am about people seeing my work before it's completed. But, so far, I'm quite pleased with it. I think that I've captured your new essence," she said.

We continued to sit with the silence being broken only by occasional car traffic outside and the constant scratching of her charcoal against the paper. I could tell that she was really concentrating now. Once in a while she would push her hair back from her face and the charcoal that was on her hands would leave smudges on her forehead. I smiled to myself and turned my thoughts to my new situation.

Before Robert had left, his comment to me made me think that he was interested in having sex with me when he returned this evening. My emotions as I thought about this possibility ranged from guilt over betraying Brad to excitement at finally being able to see what love making with Robert would be like. As the day was wearing on, and as I thought about it more, I was beginning to feel less guilt and more excitement. I had been handed an opportunity to sleep with a man whom I'd always had a yearning passion for. And although I had misgivings, I was beginning to think that the wisest course of action would be to follow my desires in this situation. I reasoned, perhaps selfishly, that I might actually be here to experience being with Robert. It didn't take me long; thinking about it, to come to the conclusion that I should embrace the opportunity to experience what being with my new husband was like. After all, if I was in Rome, then perhaps the best course of action would be to become Roman.

Coming to a resolution about the situation gave me a sense of relief for a moment. That was, until I started thinking about what being with Robert would be like. I wondered what kind of a lover he would be. As I mused about this I suddenly remembered what I had overheard the night before; when I had been out in the Jacuzzi. I realized that however well I felt that I knew Robert; I had absolutely no idea about how he was in bed.

I must have gotten a frightened look on my face as I came to this startling realization because Melissa asked, "Is something wrong? You look scared. Like you saw a ghost or something."

"No. I mean yes. I mean… No ghost. I just was thinking about what sex with Robert must be like. He sort of said that he was interested in it tonight before he left this morning. After he was harsh with me. I realized that I have no idea what he's expecting from me."

"I see," she said.

That wasn't exactly the response that I was hoping for. I was pretty sure that over the years I must have discussed my love life with Robert on at least some very minimal level, because in the past we had always discussed what sex was like with our different boyfriends in vividly lurid depth. I sat waiting for her to respond and when it was apparent that she declined to I finally asked bluntly, "I don't suppose that I've told you what being with Robert is like, have I?"

It was at that precise moment the doorbell rang. Melissa put down her sketch-pad, looked at her watch and announced, "That must be the groceries. Let's let them in. After they leave we can grab a snack and talk about your sex life, okay?"

"Sounds good to me," I said, somewhat disappointed.

We opened the door to two men who made a couple trips each, hauling up groceries. I noticed that the cleaning lady also appeared when the doorbell rang and she began putting the groceries away. Both Melissa and I helped, but I mostly watched where things went and tried to follow along, not really knowing exactly what I was doing. In fairly short order all the groceries were in their place and the cleaning woman grabbed her sweater and purse.

"Adios, missus Mary Ann," she said as she headed for the door.

"Bye," I said, happy to be alone with Melissa again.

Melissa grabbed an orange and a diet soda. She then sat down at the kitchen counter. I searched the refrigerator and came up with a piece of Colby cheese and a fruit-flavored water. Then I joined her.

"Okay, so what's the scoop about my sex life," I asked, as Melissa sat there struggling to peel her orange for a brief moment. "Out with it already. The suspense is killing me."

"Okay, but I only know the overview. You never really got into specifics about it with me. And I never really pushed you for details," she said.

"I'll take whatever I can get. If we have sex tonight and if I don't know what I'm doing, he'll know for sure that something is wrong with me," I said.

"Okay. I guess the best way to put it is that you guys like to play games. Very interesting games of dominance and submission," she said, peeking a glance at me from behind her half-peeled orange.

Her statement surprised me. I'd heard about people who played such games, but never really thought of myself as a dominatrix. As I sat there, I had visions of black high heels and a tight leather outfit fleeting through my mind. I didn't remember seeing any clothing like that up in the closet when I had gotten dressed in the morning, but I guessed it must be in a drawer or something.

"So I dress up in black leather outfits and carry a whip?" I asked, giggling at the thought.

Melissa continued to peer at me from her spot, "Not exactly."

"What do you mean, 'Not exactly'?"

"It's sort of the other way around."

"The other way around?"

"Yes. You sort of do whatever he wants."

I sat there in silence for a moment. This was rather surprising news to me. I had always considered myself to be a rather independent woman. I prided myself in being able to please my lovers while also being able to express what it was that I enjoyed having done to me when in bed. What Melissa was telling me went against the very basis of how I viewed myself. I had read about people who played such games with a passing interest, but never really had envisioned myself as being one of them. Nor had I thought that it would be much fun or pleasurable to pursue such activities.

"Are you sure about this?" I asked her.

"Yes. Very."

"I'm kind of surprised to hear this," I said. "I don't suppose that you know any details. Like exactly what it is that the two of us do?"

"I'm really sorry. But no. I really don't know. You only have ever told me that you do what he wants. Honestly, I never really wanted to know what it was that he was in to. I can tell you that, in general, you seem to enjoy it," she said.

"I guess that's a comforting thought. That I enjoy it," I said with a bit of a chuckle. "But the only thing I'm feeling about it right now is a little frightened."

"Can't say as I blame you," she said as she finished peeling the orange. She opened the bottle of soda and drank some and then pulled her orange apart and started to eat.

"Do you want to finish up the sketching?" I asked.

"Sure. As soon as I get my hands washed," she said. "And by the way, you really should make sure that you shower and brush your teeth before Robert gets home. He's made it clear that he's not happy when you smoke the clovies with me. And if you guys are going to be intimate this evening, he's going to know for sure what we've been up to."

"I see. Thanks for reminding me," I said. "I'll shower, but I think I'm going to need one more when we go back down. My nerves need a little calming here."

"No problem. That's what they're there for," she said.

We headed back down to the studio and took our previous positions. Melissa grabbed the sketchbook and began to scratch with the charcoal furiously as she drew and I knew that she was concentrating intently. I grabbed one of her cigarettes and relished the sensation of smoking it. As I inhaled I considered what I had been told. I weighed whether I still wanted to have sex or not with Robert tonight, given what I had just found out. Although I was uneasy with the situation I knew that if I didn't take this opportunity to find out what being with him was like, that I would regret it for the rest of my life. I'd spent years fantasizing about him and now that I was given the chance to make those fantasies a reality, I knew that I had to proceed forward or live with the regret forever. But something was still nagging at me from the back of my mind. What was it that we did together and would I want to do it? I decided that I would behave as though I wanted to have sex with him this evening, but I would play it by ear if things got a little too intense.

Suddenly Melissa stopped what she was doing and announced, "There. I'm finished. You better get upstairs and take your shower. Lydia's ride is going to be here shortly and then that nail guy is going to show up. I'll handle Lydia and make sure that she does her homework. I'll also get her a snack. Hurry."

"Thanks," I said. As I left the room I noticed that Melissa was lighting another cigarette as she stared out over the city.

CHAPTER 7

▼

It didn't take me long to shower and brush my teeth so that I no longer smelled of clove smoke. This time when I looked for clothes in the closet I decided to dress up a little more than I had earlier. I found a nice shift dress and a matching pair of high-heeled sandals to put on. I then dried my hair and applied enough make-up to look presentable. When I finished, I hurried back down to Melissa's studio only to find it empty. I retraced my steps up a floor and found Lydia and Melissa sitting at the kitchen counter, eating some apples.

"You look nice Mommy," Lydia said as she looked up.

"Why thank you very much," I replied.

"Mommy, you know something?"

"No. What?"

"We learned about families today."

"Really? That sounds interesting."

"Yes, we did. But now I don't understand something," she said. "And Lissa can't tell me the answer."

Melissa gave me an I-don't-know-what-to-tell-her look.

"Well, I don't know if I can help you either, but I'd be willing to try. If you want me to," I told her as I sat down at the table.

"Today the teacher told us that if we had brothers and sisters that they would be aunts and uncles to our children. Is that right?" she asked.

"Yes, that's pretty much true," I said, wondering where she was going with this.

"Okay. So which of you is Uncle Brad a brother to?"

I wasn't prepared for Lydia's question and I had no idea what she'd been told about the situation of how Brad came to be her 'Uncle' so I tried to answer her question as generally as possible, "Lydia, what the teacher told you is true about how people are related. But sometimes you call good family friends Aunt or Uncles as well." I thought that I'd done a pretty good job of not only answering, but also sidestepping, until she asked her next question.

"Okay. I understand that, I guess. It's sort of like when Janie's Mom got married and Janie calls him Dad now," she said. "But how exactly is Uncle Brad related to us then?"

I didn't know how to answer her question at all. I didn't want to tell her something that violated my former agreement with Brad or Robert, but since I had no idea what that agreement actually entailed, I was in a bind. And since Lydia's question was so direct, it was difficult to come up with a general response that answered it in terms she understood without really answering the question. I realized that I hadn't been a parent long enough to be good at handling these situations. As I was thinking about my response I saw that both Lydia and Melissa were staring at me, waiting for an answer. Luckily for me, it was at that precise moment that the doorbell rang.

"Lydia, that's probably the guy here to do my nails. I'd like to answer your question for you, but would you be willing to wait until later when I have some time to spend with you?" I asked.

"Okay Mommy," she said cheerfully. "Lissa, can you help me with my homework when I finish this apple?"

"No problem," Melissa said.

"Where would you recommend that I take this nail guy to? To have my nails done," I asked her.

"How about here at the dining room table. Lydia and I will be out of here shortly," she said.

"Great. I'll go and get him then," I said, heading to the outer door.

I opened the door to a man who announced himself as Frederick. He was dressed quite flamboyantly and from his gestures and mannerisms I guessed that he was gay. He was carrying a case and seemed to be in quite a bit of a hurry so I showed him up the stairs to the first floor. Melissa and Lydia had gathered their things and were heading down to the studio. Without my indicating it, Frederick put his case on the dining room table and opened it, taking out an assortment of nail polishes and other grooming instruments.

"Sit down here please," he said.

I did what I was told and was a little taken aback when he reached out and grabbed one of my hands and started inspecting it.

"Not bad. But there's room for improvement. I know just what I'm going to have you soak in," he said, reaching for a bottle and filling a bowl with the contents. "Please look at these colors and pick one for me."

I looked at the various nail polishes and picked out something that had a little color, but mostly mimicked pinkish flesh tones. He seemed satisfied with my selection and began to file and tend to one of my hands. When he finished with it I traded places with them; putting it into solution while the other hand began to get filed. When he finished he then dried off the first hand, soaked the other and began to apply a layer of clear foundation on the nails and then began to work on the colored polish.

As he quietly worked I felt somewhat self-conscious having someone else tending to my hands. I had always filed my own nails and mostly wore just clear polish. When I felt really adventurous I would give myself a French manicure, but Frederick seemed into using colors so I went with the flow of the moment. Then I remembered the phone call that I had made canceling the appointment. I figured that I had better tell him about it.

"Frederick?"

"Yes?"

"Earlier today I thought that I wasn't going to be able to make this appointment. So I called and canceled it. But then I was able to move things around to be here to meet with you. I just wanted you to know so when you got the message you'd understand what was going on."

"No problem. But if you need to cancel, please do it at the latest the night before. If I don't hear from you, you'll get charged anyway. Otherwise I cross you off my client list. Understood?" he asked.

"Yes. Understood. And thank you for taking me on as a client," I said, wanting to make sure he knew that I was appreciative of his efforts.

He finished applying the polish. Then he put another coat of something on top of the colored polish and dried the nails. When he finished he packed up his case hurriedly and headed for the door.

"See you next week. Call if you have any problems. It shouldn't chip, but you never know. Bye," he said.

I sat in the chair, afraid to use my hands. Even though he said that the polish was dry I was afraid to touch it with anything. After a while I got up and headed down the stairs. I found Melissa huddled together with Lydia, working on some spelling words.

"Melissa, what time do you think that Robert will be home tonight?" I asked.

Lydia looked up at me questioningly and announced, "Mommy, Daddy always comes home by six o'clock, unless he calls first."

Melissa nodded to me in agreement.

"Okay, then I guess I'm going to try to figure out what to make for dinner. Melissa, would you like to join us?" I asked.

"Lover, I'd love to, but I've got a date tonight. First one with this really dreamy guy. So, I'm going to need to pass. But remember, I'll stop by tomorrow afternoon. Okay?" she asked.

"Yes. I remember about tomorrow. Too bad about your date. I mean, too bad you can't stay for dinner. Hope you have a good time though. Good luck," I said.

"I can stay for about another hour and then I need to get going. I've got to get dressed for dinner. Someplace nice," she said.

"Want to borrow something to wear?" I asked.

"No, that's okay. But thanks for the offer. I have something new and I've been looking forward to having a place to wear it to," she said.

"Okay. Just drop Lydia off when you get ready to go. I'm going up to find something to cook," I said, turning to leave the room.

"Okay," I heard them both say, behind me.

When I got back to the kitchen I looked in the cupboards and the refrigerator. I also looked in the freezer and it was there that I found my inspiration for the meal. I had a large bag of shrimp and I decided to make a low-carb meal of Shrimp Alfredo with zucchini replacing the noodles. I also found a jar of palm hearts in the back of one of the cabinets and I decided to use them as an appetizer with the alfredo sauce over them as well. That along with some salad should fill everyone up, and hopefully I could turn the noodle replacement into an adventure for them. At any rate, I was going to have a good meal to eat. And I needed one given the stressful day I was having.

I decided to make the salad first and as I was searching the produce drawer for vegetables to add to the lettuce I remembered the salad that Crystal had made. I wasn't shooting for anything that elaborate, some nice friendly vegetables scattered through the lettuce would suffice for me. But thinking about that salad made me remember my life as it was before and I wondered how long it would be before I could go back there, or if I would ever get back there again. As I started to worry about it I reminded myself that I could look at this situation in one of two ways. I could see it as something like a punishment or I could look at it as an adventure. I reasoned that it would be far more pleasant to experience this as an adventure than sit around wasting my time worrying about how I got here and how I would get back. Reminding myself of this calmed me down and I got back to the business of cooking the meal.

One of my more favorite things to do was to create something interesting for other people to eat. When I finished dicing the vegetables and tearing the lettuce I realized that I was going to need a salad dressing. The only one that I could remember the recipe for was the one that I had made a couple of days ago. I got out the sour cream, mayonnaise and spices and tried to recreate it. I didn't get the spices exactly right, but through tasting and adding things, I got it close enough to be happy with it. When I finished, I put it in the refrigerator.

As I was cleaning up the fragments of vegetables off the cutting board I heard Melissa and Lydia come into the room.

"Time for me to go," Melissa said. "Lydia, take your school stuff up to your room, change your clothes and then you can come back down and watch the TV if you like."

"Okay, Lissa. I'll be right back down," she said, as she skipped out of the room.

"Thanks Melissa. You'll never know how much I appreciate you and what you did for me today. I think that I'll be able to make it through tonight and tomorrow okay now," I said.

"No problem. That's what friends are for after all. You've done the same for me, minus the missing memory thing, of course," she said. "I want to make sure that you have your cell phone with my number before I leave though." She walked over to the counter where a purse was sitting and reached in it. After a couple seconds of searching she pulled out a cell phone. "Here it is. Just press this down arrow and it will scroll through the numbers you have in memory. There I am. Under the M's for Melissa."

"Okay. Thanks. I'll call if I have any problems. I promise," I said.

"And you'll go to the doctor if your head starts hurting again, right?"

"Yes."

"Promise?"

"I promise. Please don't worry about me. I'm fine now," I said. But although I felt physically well, I was very nervous about what the evening held in store for me. "I'll tell Lydia that you said 'good bye' if you want to leave now and get ready for your date."

"Sounds good. You can tell her I'll be dropping by tomorrow as well," she said as she collected her tote and sweater from the couch, where she had dropped them.

"Will do," I said as I watched her leave toward the stairs. When the door swung closed behind her I suddenly felt very alone and vulnerable. I was on my own again, without anyone to help me out when I had questions about what was going on. I checked my watch and determined that I had about a half hour before Robert would be getting home.

I decided to get out the ingredients for the alfredo sauce and then I started to wash the zucchini. When I finished that and patted them dry I searched for a julienne potato slicer. Just when I was about to give up looking, I found one that looked like it had never been used way in the back of a drawer of odds and ends. I busied myself making long spaghetti noodle strips out of the meat of the zucchini. While I was doing this, Lydia returned to the room wearing a pair of jeans and an old wrinkled t-shirt.

"You sure that you want to wear that shirt for dinner?" I asked.

"Yes. It's clean Mommy. I pulled it out of the clean clothes basket just now."

I held back a giggle and replied, "Yes, it does look like it was just cleaned. Do you want to watch some TV now?"

"Yes Mommy I do, but shouldn't I set the table first?"

"I suppose so. Do you need any help?"

"I just need to know how many hot plates to put on the table. That's all," she said, looking somewhat suspiciously at me. "What are we having for dinner tonight?"

"I'm making something new tonight. Something that I saw in a magazine that I thought would be fun to try out," I said, trying to be convincing that we were about to do something exciting.

"But tonight is pizza night. We all love pizza night. Daddy makes sure to get home on time for pizza night," she said, looking at me disapprovingly.

"Well, Mommy thought that it was time for a change. Maybe a few changes, just to shake things up and keep us from getting dull and boring," I said. "Do you think that you can try to be a good sport and eat something new for me?"

Lydia looked down at the plates she was holding and in a sad voice said, "I guess so. I'll try."

"Good. Go ahead and set the table and then you can watch anything you want on TV."

That seemed to lift her spirits and she hurriedly set the dishes on the table, along with the silverware, some cloth napkins and place settings. Everything was coordinated and when she was done the overall effect was quite pleasing. She finished by putting two trivets on the table, one on either side of the flower arrangement that sat in the middle. Then she grabbed the remote and turned the TV on and flipped through the channels until she found a station playing cartoons.

After I saw that she had settled in I found a large skillet and put it on top of the stove. Then I opened a cabinet, where I remembered seeing cooking oils, and found a bottle of olive oil. I generously poured oil into the skillet and then joined Lydia on the couch, waiting for Robert to get home so that I could finish making the meal.

My watch indicated that he would be home in about five minutes, but as I sat there the seconds dragged by as though each one of them was an eternity. I was anxious to see him again, but I felt like a teenager waiting for her prom date to arrive. I knew that to him this would be just like any other boring evening at home with the family, but for me it was like a miracle. I was going to be able to touch him without his wondering why I was doing it. I didn't have to figure out a way to tell him how I felt. It was understood that I loved him enough to marry him, and he obviously loved me as well. The more I thought about this, the calmer I felt. This wasn't a first date for him, just for me. I thought about being able to kiss him and I found myself smiling.

My thoughts were interrupted by the sound of a door opening and I looked up to see Robert coming through the door.

"Daddy!" Lydia shouted as she ran toward him, determined to get a hug.

"Lyddie!" Robert mimicked as he swept her up off the floor, into his arms. He gave her a big kiss on the cheek and put her back down. She happily returned to the couch and started watching TV.

I wanted to run up to him and kiss him as well, but once he was there, standing in front of me, I found my usual shyness returning to haunt me. Instead I got up and headed for the kitchen, getting ready to cook the noodles and sauce. Robert gave me an inquisitive look and followed me into the kitchen. He stood in front of me and lifted my hair back from beside my face. He smiled and pulled me toward him and then he kissed me warmly. I felt a rush of self-consciousness. When his lips touched mine it almost felt like a soft electric shock was running through me and I almost lost my balance, but then he pulled away from me because the kiss was over. I was hoping that my face wasn't turning red from embarrassment.

"Feeling better, I hope?" he asked.

"Yes. Quite a bit, actually," I said.

"Good," he said, looking around the kitchen at what I was doing. "Not to be critical, but this doesn't exactly look like pizza makings."

"Good guess," I said lightly. "I saw a new recipe in a magazine and decided to try it. We can have pizza tomorrow if you don't mind. Lydia has begrudgingly agreed to the plan already," I added, hoping that having Lydia's blessing would pull some weight with him.

"What exactly are you making?" he asked hesitantly as he watched me turn on the stove burners under the two pans.

"Shrimp Alfredo over vegetable noodles, with a palm heart appetizer," I answered.

He picked up the jar of palm hearts and looked at them. "So you finally figured out what to do with these things. This should be interesting. I'm going to go upstairs to change my clothes. Be back shortly."

"No problem. It will be at least ten minutes before this will all be ready," I said.

While he was gone I mixed the ingredients for the alfredo sauce together and let it slowly warm. I heated the olive oil and then dropped the noodles in, occasionally tossing them until they became translucent. When they were done I put them in a colander and let the water drain. I also cooked the shrimp. By this time Robert returned and was standing in the kitchen, looking at what I was doing. Even though I felt a little nervous with him watching, I continued what I was doing with ease. I opened the jar of palm hearts and put them on appetizer plates, then poured some of the alfredo sauce over them. The rest of the sauce I put in a bowl. Then I got out two more bowls and poured the noodles and shrimp into each, respectively. At this point I asked Robert to put the food on the table while I went to get the salad and the dressing out of the refrigerator.

"Time for dinner Lydia," I said.

Lydia came bouncing over to the table from the couch and eyed the meal suspiciously. In fact, both of them had the same look on their faces; only Robert's was a little more masked because of his maturity. I softly giggled and both of them looked at me as though they were wondering if I was playing some sort of a joke on them. I sat down and picked my knife and fork up and began to cut the palm heart into bite-sized pieces. Then I popped one of them into my mouth. Both of them seemed to relax and started to eat theirs as well.

"Not bad," Robert said.

"Yeah Mommy. Not bad," Lydia said as well.

When we all had finished the appetizer I showed them how to assemble their main meal; first putting the noodles on my plate, then the shrimp topped off with the alfredo sauce. They both dutifully followed my lead and began to eat.

"This is pretty good too. Where did you find this recipe? What kind of food is this?" he asked.

Actually, it's from low carbohydrate menus. Looked very interesting to me so I thought that we could try it," I said.

"It makes a nice change," he said. "And speaking of change. I noticed that something is different upstairs in the bedroom. Care to elaborate?"

It took me a minute to remember what he was talking about, and then I recalled that Melissa and I had replaced the painting up there.

"Oh, the painting. Isn't it beautiful? Melissa painted it for me as a birthday gift. It's the most beautiful thing I've ever seen and I thought that it looked great up there in our bedroom. Matched perfectly," I said, realizing that I was beginning to ramble because I was nervous. "I decided that I wanted to start every day looking at it," I said, trying to wrap up my thoughts.

"Could you pass the salad and dressing?" he asked. As I moved both of them to within his reach he continued, "Yes, it is nice and it does go with the room nicely, but the other painting was specifically picked out for that room. It was also quite expensive and we're still making payments on it."

"I thought about that," I said, congratulating myself on the nice recovery. "But I really like the one that Melissa painted. I put the other one upstairs in the office. I figure that maybe we can use it somewhere else in the house. Or, if you really like it, maybe you can put it up in your office. If worse comes to worst, perhaps we could get our money back from selling it."

"This is the salad dressing?" he asked, pointing to the bowl in front of him.

"Yes, actually it is. I made it myself," I replied.

"Do we have our regular bottled dressing?"

"Yes, but I thought that you could try something new. I'll get the other dressing if you need it."

"No, that's okay. I'll try this," he said as he spooned some of it out of the bowl and poured it over his salad. Once he had finished he ate a forkful of the salad. "This is actually pretty good. Tastes fresher than the bottled stuff."

"I like it too," Lydia chimed in agreement.

"Thank you," I said.

"But getting back to the painting. I can appreciate the fact that you want to put up the gift from Melissa, but I'm a little taken aback that you made the decision, unilaterally, to put it up in that spot. I can live with your decision, but I'd like to be consulted about such things in the future. Agreed?" he asked.

"I guess so," I said. "But I really like the painting there. It makes me feel something very special when I look at it, and I want to feel that way every morning when I wake up. I just love it. Don't you?"

"I think that it's lovely, but I don't have the same reaction to it that you do. I'll try to get used to it and I'll call the art gallery owner and see what we can do to resell the one you replaced. I seem to recall his telling me that there was some interest in it after I purchased it originally," he said.

"That's great," I said, feeling very relieved that this wasn't going to become a big issue that needed to be discussed more in-depth. "It's not that I don't like the other painting. It's just that I absolutely love the one that Melissa made for me."

The rest of the meal went very smoothly. Lydia told us what happened during her day at Robert's prodding. Both of them seemed to like the food enough to finish eating all of it. Lydia was a little concerned about the zucchini noodles, but after she poured enough alfredo sauce over them that she couldn't see the green anymore, she happily ate it all. After we finished, Robert reminded her that she needed a bath and to get ready for bed. I accompanied her upstairs and got her tub ready. She seemed content to play with her water toys and after a while I heard her singing to herself. I told her to change into the pajamas that I found in her room and to come downstairs when she was finished. She gave me an 'of course' look and I headed back for the living area.

I opened the door to our first floor and saw Robert standing near the front window, drinking what appeared to be a goblet of wine as he looked out over the city. It was beginning to become dusk and the city was sprinkled with lights turning on. When he heard me, he turned around and pointed to another full wine glass that was sitting on the coffee table in front of the couch. I picked it up and sat down on the couch. I looked at him silhouetted against the view of the city and was reminded of when I watched him as the sun had set the night before. This time he seemed more at peace. As I looked at him the old longing to touch him, that I had lived with for years, returned. I smiled, took a drink of the wine, noting that it tasted quite nice. Then I walked up behind him and put my arms around him, resting my cheek on the back of his shoulder.

He slowly turned around and looked at me with a smile. He put his arms around me as well and we just stood there for a few moments holding each other. I knew that he wasn't really upset with me about the painting anymore because I could feel that his touch was accepting of me. After a couple of minutes we parted and I sat down again on the couch and picked up my wine glass.

"I like this. What is it?" I asked.

"It's one of the merlots that we picked up when we went wine tasting last fall."

"Quite nice. By the way, I left Lydia in the bath and told her to put her pajamas on and to come back down once she was done."

"Good. We can let her watch a little TV and then I'll read her a book until she goes to sleep," he said. "Then we can plan what we're going to tell Brad about taking her away to visit his parents."

"While we are at it," I said, remembering my earlier conversation with Lydia. "We should also talk about what to tell Lydia about her relationship to Brad. She learned about families in school today and who Uncles are and was asking questions earlier. I didn't want to say anything until I talked to you about it."

"We'll just have to put her off about it until we talk to Brad about things tomorrow. He's going to take her to the zoo and then she's going to a birthday party at Carole's so we'll have plenty of time to talk things over," he said.

"Sounds interesting," I said honestly enough. It would be very educational to see how Brad and Robert interacted with each other when we all got together. I was planning on remaining fairly quiet in order to learn as much as I could about how this situation, concerning Lydia, worked.

I took another sip of the wine and then Lydia returned, dressed in her pajamas. She knowingly went over to the TV and turned it on. Robert turned the overhead lights off and we all sat on the couch in the semi-darkness and watched a repeat of a sit-com on the Nickelodeon Channel. When it was over Robert told her to head upstairs and to get the book that they were reading. She agreed and skipped off toward the stairs to her room.

After she left the room Robert turned to me, "Why don't you go upstairs and put something more comfortable on. I liked the purple satin PJs that you had on last night if you're in the mood to wear them again."

"Okay," I said as he turned and followed Lydia out of the room.

It was at that moment that the reality of the situation really hit home. I thought of putting the pajamas on and then being in the same room with Robert and I suddenly felt like I would feel naked in that situation. And worse yet, I would actually have to get naked with him shortly after that if I wanted to have sex with him. It seemed as much an invasion of his privacy for me to see him naked as I felt that it was an invasion of my privacy to get naked in front of him. And as I sat there thinking about it I wasn't sure which I was more afraid of. I finally decided to go upstairs and get changed. I would concentrate on how much I wanted to be with him and how I would be able to touch him and be touched by him in order to get over my panic from being thrown into this sudden intimacy. I remembered that I needed to be calm, act as though I was used to being his wife, because in his eyes I had been his wife for years. In fact, for him this would just be another usual evening spent with a woman who he probably had gotten bored with by now. I needed to try to act as though this was the usual thing for me as well, if I could.

It didn't take me long to get upstairs where I found and put on the pajamas that I had woke up in this morning. Although I wasn't wild about the color of them, I did like the texture of the satin against my skin and they had a nice loose fit that I hadn't noticed during the confusion earlier in the day. I also took off my jewelry and put it in the container where I had found it. I then ran a hairbrush through my hair and checked my make-up. Normally I would take my make-up off, but I was far too self-conscious to let Robert see what I looked like without at least a little mascara and powder on.

Having finished, I headed back down to the living area and sat on the couch taking small sips of my wine. It was almost surreal sitting there in the half darkness looking out over the inky black of the night speckled by the lights from the buildings and the bridges that I could see. I sat watching the world bustling below me, people living their lives, not knowing or caring that I was an onlooker here in the safety of my home. After a little while I heard Robert coming down the stairs and soon he opened the door and entered the room. He retrieved his wine glass and topped it off with the open bottle that was sitting on the kitchen counter. He held the bottle up, motioning toward my glass in an effort to determine if I wanted a top off too. I nodded; he brought the bottle over and carefully filled my glass.

"Let's keep the lights low, if you don't mind," I said. "I just love the peaceful feeling of watching the city lights below."

He didn't say anything. Instead he put the bottle down on the coffee table and sat beside me. Together we sat looking out the window onto the world below us.

After a while he finally spoke, "Do you have a problem letting Lydia spend some time with Brad when he goes to see his parents?"

"Not really. As long as she wants to go with him I don't see that we need to make an issue out of it," I answered.

"Good. I think that it's best for her to go with him as well. I just wasn't sure that you'd feel okay with her being gone for over a week. She's never been gone longer than overnights at her friends. This will be quite an adjustment for all of us," he said.

"I think that she's old enough, but I just want to be sure that it's something that she feels comfortable doing. That's all," I said, feeling quite motherly toward her all of a sudden.

"Good. That's settled then. Now we just need to talk to Brad tomorrow about what to tell Lydia about her trip, as well as her relationship to him," he said as he reached over and held my hand.

"Robert?"

"Yes?"

"Why didn't you ever ask for a paternity test to see whose child Lydia is?" I asked with a little hesitation. "I sometimes wonder how you can go on not really knowing the answer to that question. I know that I'm quite curious about it."

Robert sat quietly in the darkness for a little while longer and then he calmly began to speak. "Lydia is my daughter. Whether or not we have the same DNA. We have raised her. I also can tell from her mannerisms and the way that she looks that she's mine."

"I think that you're right," I said. "But wouldn't it be better for everyone if we finally ended the uncertainty of this situation and found out for sure?"

"Perhaps. But it's not what we all agreed to. When all of this began, I wanted you and you were torn between the two of us. And let's not forget that Brad wanted you too and didn't want to give up a child that he thought could be his. As unlivable as this situation has turned out to be, it was your idea of a compromise. Everyone got a child and you and I got to be together," he said. "I know that I agreed to it because it was what you seemed to want at the time and it was the only way that I could be certain to get you. If the test had turned out that Lydia was Brad's child I would have lost you forever. It wasn't a risk I was willing to take; it's still not something that I'm willing to gamble with."

"I see." I certainly couldn't argue with logic like that. "There's something else that I've been thinking about lately. I was thinking about that night that I came over to see you, after Brad and I got into that fight. The night that we slept together for the first time. I was wondering what it was that I did to make you know that I wanted to be with you. Do you recall?"

I could hear him chuckle lightly next to me. "That's simple. You did something unexpected. When I asked you if you wanted to talk to Brad, when he called, you told me 'no.' I remember thinking, while I was telling him that you weren't there, that it wasn't like you to not take his call, no matter how angry you were. After I hung up with him I asked you why you had told me to lie to him. You broke down and told me how you felt about me, how you had been hiding your feelings for so long."

"That was pretty brave of me," I said, thinking that it really was.

"Yes. Because once you told me how you felt, I was free to tell you how I felt as well. I had always had romantic feelings for you, but Brad was my friend and frankly the two of you always seemed so happy together. So perfect. I honestly didn't think that I had a chance so I just tried to put my feelings out of my mind and was contented to be your friend. You always were a good friend."

"You were a good friend too. But, I'm glad that I did something out of character then. Things seem to have worked out okay," I said. "Lydia is a beautiful and happy child. She seems very well adjusted."

"I think that you're right about Lydia. And I'm thankful that you so shamelessly came on to me that night," he said jokingly as he took the glass from my hand and put it on the coffee table in front of us. He put his hand on the back of my head and pulled me toward him and into a rather passionate kiss. As we were kissing I was thankful that our relationship hadn't gotten so routine that a little foreplay was out of the question. He seemed to genuinely be enjoying the challenge of getting me excited before we got more seriously into the act of sex. After we spent some time making out like teenagers he said, "What do you say about us going upstairs where I can slip into something as comfortable as what you have on?"

"Sounds good," I said without thinking. As he handed me back my wine glass and topped it off with what was left in the bottle, I again began to feel some pangs of guilt about being unfaithful to Brad. But when Robert returned from getting another bottle of wine from the kitchen and grabbed my hand I let those feelings go. He energetically pulled me out of the room and up the stairs to the bedroom and with each step I took I left my old life a little further behind.

Once we reached the master bedroom he turned on some dim recessed lighting that allowed me to see where I was going, but wouldn't allow people to see in. I was happy that he didn't head straight for the switch that would have closed the wall of curtains so that I couldn't see the city lights.

"Why don't you get in bed and I'll be back in a moment," he said.

That seemed fine to me so I followed him to the bed, where he deposited his wine glass and bottle on the nightstand. He then headed for the closet and I got into the bed awaiting his return. I took another gulp of the wine and could feel that I was definitely getting a little tipsy from all the drinking I had done so far. I didn't have an accurate count of how many glasses I'd consumed because every time I would drink some, Robert would top me off. As I sat there feeling warm and fuzzy inside I wondered if getting me drunk was part of his plan for the evening. I didn't have long to ponder the question because it was about that time that he returned from the closet, as naked as the day that he was born. I noticed in the half lighting that he was slightly erect as he walked across the room and I smiled thinking that even after all the years we had been together, it seemed that he still found me attractive and was aroused by the thought of being with me.

When he reached the bed, instead of getting in, Robert opened the drawer in the nightstand. It didn't take him long to pull out what looked like a small black leather belt and a couple lengths of rope. He laid them on the bed beside me and said, "Put that on while I check to make sure that the doors are locked and the security system is activated. You can get undressed now too." He walked over to a panel on the wall near the stairway door and I saw him press several buttons and then I heard him mutter, "That's good. Now we can hear Lydia too." I assumed that there must have been an audio monitor that he had activated. While he was turning the security system on I looked at the items placed beside me and wasn't certain what I was supposed to 'put on' or how I was supposed to do it. When he got back to the bed and noticed my inaction he seemed rather puzzled.

"Didn't you hear what I said?"

"Yes. I heard you…"

"Well, why didn't you put your collar on?" he asked. Suddenly I understood that the little leather belt was supposed to be worn as a collar. I slowly reached for it, wanting to please him, but not being sure exactly how I was to do that.

He must have noticed my hesitance because he continued, "If you don't want to stay up we can call it a night, but I thought we made plans." He reached for the collar, taking it from my hands and returned it to the drawer.

"What do you mean?" I asked.

"I mean, if you don't want to wear it then we can just go to sleep," he said, fumbling for the ropes on the bed and returning them to the drawer as well.

"I don't want to just go to sleep. I want to be with you tonight," I said, somewhat confused.

"If you want to fuck tonight, then you need to put on that collar and start following the rules," he said as he retrieved the collar and laid it beside me again on the bed.

I reached over for the collar and held it in my hands, feeling the smooth leather finish on one side and the roughness of the unfinished side. "What if I want to be with you, but I'm just not in the mood to wear this?" I asked.

"So you're playing the coy princess this evening?" he asked.

That seemed accurate enough, although I probably would have described it more as the confused princess. "No…" I started.

"Look, it's like I told you from the very first night that we spent together," he said. "If you're going to be with me, I need to know that you're mine totally and completely. I need for you to give yourself over to me in every way. And that includes putting on that collar and following the rules. I have no interest in sex with you if you're only half-heartedly into it."

I sat staring down at the collar in my hands as he watched me in the darkness. I really did want to be with him. And I was finding, as the night progressed, that I was finding pleasure in wanting to please him. But the idea of 'giving myself over completely' was scaring me, especially since I wasn't sure that I was interested in finding out what the ropes he had put on the bed were used for. In my mind it took a lot of trust in someone to blindly do what they asked and even more trust to let them tie you up and then do what they wanted. I wasn't sure how much trust I could muster up during a first time, for me, sexual encounter. On the other hand, I reasoned, I had known Robert for many years and I did trust him on many levels.

"Can I wear this, but ask for you not to tie me up tonight? Remember, I haven't been feeling all that well today," I asked.

"I guess that I can do that, but all the other rules are in effect," he said. "But this is interesting… My coy princess usually likes to be tied up most of all." He reached over to me and gently lifted my hair waiting for me to put the collar on.

I tried to put the collar around my neck, but it really did feel odd. I fed the rounded leather end through the metal buckle and finally got it on. He let my hair fall and leaned over and kissed me on the neck, right above the collar and with one of his hands he felt the collar. He then leaned back and said, "It needs to be tighter. Tighten it up. Drink some more wine. And take those pajamas off."

As I fumbled again with the collar, trying to clasp it tighter he began to talk. "Let's go over the rules since you seem to be in an odd mood this evening. You do what you're told, when you're told, without complaint. In fact, you don't talk unless spoken to. When you are spoken to you respond with respect. I like to be called Mr. Monroe. Do you understand?"

"Yes."

"Yes, what?"

I thought for a moment and realized my mistake, "Yes, Mr. Monroe."

"That's better," he said. "Any infraction of these rules will lead to punishment. Punishment that I decide given my whim of the moment. Understood?"

"Yes, Mr. Monroe."

"And don't forget your safeword. If things get to be too much for you, you can say 'bergma' and we'll totally stop what we are doing and go to sleep for the night," he continued.

I finally got the collar as tight as I could while still being able to breathe. I could put two fingers underneath it. I reached for my glass of wine and felt Robert reach up and tug on the collar as I drank. I decided to finish off the glass figuring that being a little more drunk wouldn't hurt in this situation. As I returned the glass to its place on the nightstand I felt Robert's hand drop from my neck to my arm and he began gently rubbing his hand up and down my satin sleeve. He softly said, "Good. That's tight enough. Lie down."

As my nervousness at getting naked with him began to build I looked down at his bare body lying on the bed beside me and reminded myself that he'd seen my body hundreds of times during the seven years that we'd been married. He wouldn't think twice about how I looked, even if he cared to notice. So I slowly unbuttoned the front of the pajama top and let it fall onto the bed. He picked it up and tossed it on the floor. I then pulled down the bottoms and he deposited them in the same place as well. As I laid down on the bed beside him I felt him turn toward me and then he began to kiss me.

I managed to get through the experience without receiving any of the punishment that he had talked about. I found him to be a considerate lover, but he knew what he wanted and when he wanted it. I found myself happy to comply with his wishes and knowing that I didn't really have a choice sort of made the experience more intense than I was used to. I was also surprised by how he knew what would excite me, and what wouldn't. He spent a lot of time doing things that I found immensely pleasurable, some of which I had no idea that I would like. I had always prepared myself for being disappointed if I ever had gotten the chance to be with him because in my experience first time sexual encounters were usually a disaster. But instead, I got a consummate, if not somewhat frightening lover.

When we were done I rolled over onto my back and softly muttered, "Thanks."

Robert quickly rolled toward me and placed his finger on my lips to silence me. "Shush," he said quietly. "You don't want me to have to punish you now, do you?"

"No, Mr. Monroe," I replied dutifully.

He then loosened the collar around my neck. "Now you can thank me all that you like, my coy little princess."

After he put the collar back into the drawer beside the bed he rolled back over and put his arms around me. I could hear his breathing becoming more regular and I knew that he was beginning to fall asleep. I was pretty tired so I let myself relax in his arms. As I felt myself falling asleep the thought crossed my mind that it would be all too easy to lose myself in the presence of this man. No wonder I had ugly purple velvet curtains that I hated. Obviously Robert had a fondness for them and I had wanted to please him. At this moment I would have granted him purple curtains with pink polka dots if he requested it of me.

CHAPTER 8

▼

The next morning I woke up to the sound of a door being opened.

"Good. You're finally awake princess. I decided to bring you up a cup of coffee to help get you going this morning," Robert said as he brought a large mug over to the nightstand beside me. "Lydia has already left for the zoo with Brad, who as usual, was right on time."

"Oh. Okay. Thanks," I said, trying to pull myself further into total consciousness.

"How are you feeling this morning? Need some aspirin or something?"

Actually I felt pretty good considering how much wine I had drank the night before, but I could feel the slight tinge of a hangover so I accepted his offer. Robert went into the bathroom and I heard him open the medicine cabinet and then close it. He brought me two aspirin and sat down on the bed beside me.

"Decaf?" I asked, pointing toward the coffee cup.

"Nope. Just your usual high-octane stuff. Sumatra, if memory serves."

"Thanks," I said again, as I popped the pills into my mouth and took a sip of the coffee.

"No problem. I'm even available this morning for some major breakfast cooking if you're interested. After last night's adventure in eating I figured that I owed you something. However, I'm going to have to stick to my regular menu selections, if you don't mind. So what are you in the mood for on this beautiful day?" he said as he swung his arm toward the glass wall that was pouring in the sun from the gorgeous day that had begun outside.

"Would an omelet be on your limited menu?" I asked.

"Yep. The kitchen can handle that request," he said. "What would you like in your 'well cooked' omelet this fine morning?"

"Humm," I said, thinking. "How about some Colby or Monterey Jack cheese with some tomatoes or salsa with something else, like avocado or bell peppers?"

"I think that I could rustle that up for you. What kind of toast would you like?" he asked.

"No toast and no hash browns," I said.

"You don't want my world-famous hash browns this morning?" he asked in amazement.

"Don't think so," I said. "I'm still a little queasy from the wine last night. But if you want to make some bacon or ham, I might be able to eat some of that."

"Okay. I'm in the mood for bacon myself."

"Crispy," we both said in unison.

"I know. I know. You know how I like my bacon cooked," I said.

"I should after all these years, don't you think? I also have it burned in my memory to cook the eggs on both sides before I put the goodies in. Don't worry fair princess, you're in good hands this morning," he said, getting up and walking toward the door. "Oh yes," he said, turning around. "Do you want to eat up here or downstairs?"

"I think it's time for me to get up, don't you?" I said. "I'll take a quick shower when I finish this coffee and meet you in the kitchen. If that's okay with you."

"Meet you downstairs when you get done. It should take me fifteen or twenty minutes to put our food together," he said, and then he turned and left the room.

I drank down the rest of the coffee, which really was helping to wake me completely up. Then I showered and got dressed, again in a summer-time long tank dress. The one I found this morning had flowers on it and had a matching cardigan that I tied over my shoulders. I found myself wishing that the closet held more of these casual, nice outfits instead of all the business attire that was hanging there. A little more searching located another pair of sandals that were a little dressier, with heels. I then put on my wedding ring set and located an armoire that had a lot of different jewelry in it. I picked out a couple of small, tasteful pieces and put them on as well. After I ran a comb and brush through my hair, I touched up my appearance with some foundation powder, mascara and lipstick. I felt ready to head on downstairs.

When I opened the door to the living area I could see that Robert was in full swing, making breakfast for me. Everything that he was using was still out of the refrigerator, on the counter, and he was busy flipping the omelet eggs, making sure that they were cooked before putting the cheese on it.

"I'm going to use both Colby and Jack cheese. I hope that's okay as I'm in the mood for both myself this morning," he said.

I nodded in agreement and sat down at the kitchen counter, where I could spend time with him as he worked.

"Don't worry. I'm in charge of clean up this morning too," he said, sprinkling the cheese over the cooked eggs. "Enough? Or do you want more cheese?"

"Just a little more," I said. "So when is Brad coming back with Lydia? And are we going to have our little pow-wow when they get back?"

"They should get back in less than two hours. And we can conference together after I get back from taking her to the party. It's just over on the next hill so you'll only have to spend about thirty minutes here alone with him. Is that okay? Or should I take him with me to drop her off?" he asked.

"No. I'm okay with him here."

"Your choice."

I watched as he folded the eggs over the cheese, avocado and bell peppers. Then he lifted it onto a plate, next to a couple of pieces of bacon, and handed it, as well as a jar of salsa to me.

"You can eat here now or wait until I cook mine and we can go more formal in the dining room," he said.

"I'll wait for you," I said and busied myself opening the salsa and spooning out some of it over my omelet.

It didn't take him long to cook his omelet as it appeared that he wasn't as concerned about thoroughly cooking it as I was. Once he finished, he poured both of us a cup of coffee and then we headed over to the dining room table and sat down to eat. The omelet was cooked perfectly and tasted very good. It seemed that he had put some garlic and other seasonings in the egg before I had gotten to the kitchen and the tastes combined together were really very unique and good.

"Excellent," I said.

"Me thanks my fair princess," he said with a smile. We sat quietly eating for a while and then he said, "I'll call the gallery when we get done here and find out how to put our newly orphaned painting back on the market."

"That sounds good. It would be great if we could resell it," I said.

"I looked at Melissa's masterpiece up there more closely this morning," he said. "I actually like it better than I thought I did last night. The flowers really make it look like it belongs in the room. It gives me a little empty, sad feeling, but I'll have to admit that it's pleasing to the eye. And if you like it, I'll try to adjust. After all, we don't need Melissa angry at us. She's so good with Lydia."

"Yes she is, isn't she," I said. "That reminds me. She's coming over to work later on this afternoon. I told her that I'd spend a little time with her if that's okay."

"Shouldn't be a problem. I planned on picking Lydia up after her party and then I need to run my Saturday errands. I've got to get some shirts at the cleaners or I'm going to be going to work in t-shirts next week. Not exactly the confidence-instilling outerwear clients want to see their attorney in, if you catch my drift. I also might stop by the gallery if they need me to fill out any paperwork or drop off the painting. You should have plenty of time to chat with Melissa and reassure her that I don't hate her painting," he said. "But remember not to bother her too much, or she'll never get any work done down there."

After we finished eating he got up and began to tidy up the mess that he'd made in the kitchen. As I continued to eat my omelet I watched him. He was only wearing a pair of jeans and a blue shirt patterned with tan and green, but he looked very sensual to me. I noticed that he had finished off his look with matching brown leather accessories, a belt, shoes and a watch, but it was something more than that. The shirt brought out the blue color in his eyes, making them seem even more intense than usual, but what I was noticing was his movements. He had a certain grace that made him appear to be confident. I wondered if his clients trusted his advice more because of this quality. A quality that I guessed he didn't even know that he had. Although, remembering back, perhaps this was the reason that I had been attracted to him that first time I had seen him walking by.

When I finished the food on my plate, I took it into the kitchen and put it in the dishwasher. After that I poured myself yet another cup of coffee and headed back to the couch. As I looked out onto the city below me I noticed that a ceiling of clouds was beginning to form way up above us, somewhat blocking out the sun. It was still very bright, but if the cloud cover got thicker we certainly would begin to feel the weather getting gloomier.

"I've done my work here," Robert said. "I'm going up to the office to make that call. I'll keep an ear out for when Brad gets here with Lydia."

"Okay. I'm fine now," I said.

Looking out the window I noticed that there was a delivery truck pulled up on the street in front of the house. There were two men taking a refrigerator out of it by means of a hydraulic lift. I watched as they lowered it to street level from the truck bed. Then they strapped it to an appliance dolly and started pulling it toward one of the houses below. As I watched I noticed a black SUV had pulled up right below and a little girl stepped out of it. She was holding a purple balloon. When I looked at her more closely she seemed familiar and then I realized that it was Lydia. I instantly recognized Brad when he opened the driver's door and got out. From my vantage point it seemed that he looked much the same as I remembered him. He too, was dressed in jeans and was wearing a tan colored polo shirt. I watched as he followed Lydia to the house.

It didn't take long for me to hear Lydia climbing the stairs, talking to Brad the whole time. Then the door opened and they came in.

"Mommy, see the pretty balloon that Uncle Brad bought me?"

"Yes. I do. That's really very nice," I said. "And did you remember to thank him for it?"

"She did," Brad said. "She was very well behaved."

"Okay," I said. "Be careful Lydia. If you let it go it will fly up to the ceiling and we won't be able to get it back down."

"No Mommy. It has one of these," she said, pointing to a black plastic-looking disc attached to the end of the string. With that she purposefully let go of it and the disc gently pulled the balloon down toward the ground.

"Why that's quite neat," I told her. "I've never seen one of those before."

Both of them gave me a questioning look and I instantly knew that I must have seen one of these discs before in their presence. "That's an interesting shape," I said, hoping that might explain my previous statement at least enough to keep them from questioning me.

At that moment Robert entered the room, "Perfect timing. I should just be able to get Lydia to her party in time."

"Good," Brad said. "I was worried that I'd be a little late. Ran into some traffic on the way over here. Strange, because usually it's pretty good on the weekends."

"Well, all's well that ends well," Robert said. "Lydia, put your stuff up in your room and let's get going."

"Okay Daddy," she said, heading toward the door. Then she stopped and turned, "Thank you Uncle Brad. I had a fun time." And then she turned and headed upstairs.

"Sounds like the two of you had a good time," I said.

"I always enjoy my time with her. I like to see the world through her eyes," Brad said.

"Brad, it will take me about a half hour, at the most, to get back from dropping Lydia off. Mary Ann says that it's fine if you want to stay here and wait. Or you can come with me," Robert said. "We're still on schedule for our discussion today."

"I'll stay here if Mary Ann really doesn't mind," Brad said, looking at me.

"No problem," I said.

"Then it's settled," Robert said. "I'll go track down Lydia. I'll be back shortly."

After Robert left I turned to Brad. "You can have a seat if you want. I'm having some coffee. Would you like some too?"

"Yes, that would be okay," he said with a little shrug of his shoulders that told me that he could have cared less about what I gave him to drink.

Suddenly I felt rather nervous being around him. He looked the same, but there was something definitely different about him. I was glad that he wanted coffee because it gave me something to do. "Regular or Decaf?" I asked.

"Regular, of course," he said. "And that strong stuff that you like will be fine."

"You mean the Sumatra?"

"Yeah, whatever."

Just what I needed today was some more caffeinated coffee I thought to myself. On the other hand, why not? Over the past day I had indulged in just about all of my favorite vices; cigarettes, liquor, caffeine, not to mention my favorite fantasy, Robert. What harm could a little more caffeine do at this point? It didn't take long for the water to start falling through the coffee grounds. When the carafe was about half full I poured a mug full and took it over to Brad. He was sitting on the couch quietly looking out the window.

"Here you go," I said, sitting the mug on the coffee table in front of him.

"Thanks."

"So you and Lydia had fun today?"

"Yes. I enjoy her company," he said. "She really liked the lions. We had to go back and see them again before we left." When he finished speaking he turned his attention again to looking out the window.

"It's quite the view, isn't it?" I asked.

Brad gave me a pained look. "You're different today. Did you change your hair or something?"

"Maybe a little," I said. "I'm sorry. I just feel like talking. Do you mind?"

"No, I guess not," he said. "It certainly will pass the time quicker."

"I've just been thinking a lot about the past lately. Going over things. I guess that this proposal of yours, taking Lydia to see your parents, has me doing some soul searching," I said, hoping that my explanation seemed reasonable to him.

"I didn't mean to make you uncomfortable by asking to spend time with her," he said. "I would just like to see her more than a couple of hours a month. I want to get to know her better, and so do my parents."

"I can understand that," I said. "But this arrangement that we all have certainly is fraught with complications."

"Tell me about it," he said, looking down at his coffee.

"Just so you know. Lydia has begun asking questions about your family relationship to her. They went over what an 'Uncle' is in school this week and she came home with an armful of questions about it," I said.

"What did you tell her?"

"Nothing yet. I put her off until the three of us could talk about it. That's on the agenda today as well. Just a head's up."

"What does Robert want to tell her?"

"He didn't say. He just said that we should talk about it today."

"Okay. Fair enough."

"By the way, have you ever reconsidered our plan?" I asked. "I mean, have you ever wanted to have a paternity test done in order to find out who Lydia's biological father is?"

Brad gave me a quick angry look, got up and walked toward the window. In one movement he had managed to put as much distance as possible in the room between us. Then he turned and said, "So I see what this is all about. You don't bother to have a real conversation with me for seven years. And now that you want something, all of a sudden you're friendly. What happened? Did you have a secret paternity test done so that you know that she's Robert's and now you want to cut me out of your lives?"

"No. That's not it. Really," I said.

But Brad didn't seem to hear me because as he turned to face the window he continued, "From that first time that you were with Robert, you changed. I remember when you came home that morning with some story about having stayed over at a girlfriend's house. You were so distant, not letting me touch you. Not talking to me. It didn't come as a big surprise when you told me a couple of weeks later that you were pregnant and that you didn't know who the father was. However I *was* surprised to find out who you'd been with."

"Brad, please stop," I said, walking toward him. I put my hand on his shoulder, trying to bring his attention back to the present. But when he felt my touch he pulled away and turned to face me.

"Don't. Don't touch me," he said.

"Sorry, I didn't mean to startle you. I just want you to talk to me," I said. "Remember a couple of minutes ago when you said that you thought that I was different? Well, for the sake of argument, let's say that I am. And let's say that I'm not trying to hurt you as well. Can we do that?"

Brad stood there staring at me, not willing to commit to my premise.

So I continued, "This arrangement that we all have can't help but be painful for everyone. I can totally understand your frustration with how things have happened and how you're being made to live. I was thinking about that and about how you must be feeling. That's why I asked you that question. I swear that I don't have any devious motives."

He seemed to relax a little as I talked.

"I'm worried about what we're going to tell Lydia," I continued. "I'm worried about her and I'm worried about both you and Robert. I've been thinking a lot about our situation, trying to see if there isn't some better solution than the one that we're all living with. I just wanted to know how you felt about all of this ambiguity. And, I guess that your anger answers my question. I thought that you might be happier knowing whether or not she really was your daughter. If she's not, then you wouldn't have to live your life around these weekend drives up here."

"I don't mind coming here to see her," he said. "And if the tests showed that she was mine I'd be torn between the selfish thing of wanting to have equal or total custody of her and the better thing for her of letting her stay here with the two of you. At this point I think that a paternity test would cause more problems for all of us, rather than solve any."

"That's interesting," I said.

"What is?" he asked.

"It seems that both you and Robert are in agreement about this. Neither of you are interested in determining the exact paternity of Lydia," I said. "I just thought that knowing the truth would clear up things for everyone. Make it better."

"Don't feel too bad Mary Ann," he said. "Over the years I've often thought that we should do the tests too. But when I think about how I'd feel if the tests turned out negative for me, I know that I don't want to. Lydia reminds me of how you used to be; independent, self-assured and mostly happy all the time. She's the only link I still have to that life I could have had, if you hadn't left me for Robert. Whether or not she's mine, I do know she has the parts of you that I cherished most in her and I love her for that. I don't mind being her part-time dad, no matter how painful it is sometimes."

"I see. At least everyone is pretty much in agreement about this. I don't think that it will be too difficult to work things out when Robert gets back," I said. "So, if you don't mind. Tell me about your wife. She doesn't come to visit Lydia too often. Do the two of them get along okay?"

"So far they do. I didn't want to complicate our first year of marriage by mixing Lydia into our lives too quickly. So I've been gradually letting the two of them spend time together. She'll be coming along, to visit my parents, if that's not a problem for you," he said.

"I can only speak for myself, but as long as you're comfortable with it I don't see it as a problem. Are you planning to have more children in the near future?" I asked.

"We're working on it. Spending time with Lydia has given me an appreciation for having children. Plus I think that it would be good for her to have a sister or brother," he said.

"Well, it sounds like things are really working out for you," I said. "You've made a comfortable life for yourself here."

"Yes. I have."

"Well, I think that if we had stayed together we would have been very happy as well. But it's good to see that you've created an existence that gives you peace and contentment," I said.

Brad looked at me and smiled. We walked back over to the couch and sat down.

"Want some more coffee?" I asked.

"Sure. Why not? I still have a fair drive to make home when we get done talking. I can use the caffeine," he said.

I got up with both of our mugs and topped them off from the carafe in the kitchen. At about that time I heard Robert.

"Sorry that took so long," he said. "I just couldn't drop her off and run because Carole wanted to chat about Lydia's teacher's bridal shower and what we should all contribute to it. But I managed to escape when the next parent arrived."

"No problem," Brad said. "We were actually having a meaningful conversation."

Robert gave me a questioning look as he entered the kitchen in search of a mug to fill with coffee for himself.

"Yes. Brad and I were discussing our past as well as his life with his present wife," I said. "It appears that she and Lydia are learning to get along well."

"That sounds promising," Robert said. "So is everyone ready to call our meeting to order?"

"Yes," I said, trying to sound upbeat.

Brad nodded in agreement.

"So, the first order of business is whether or not Brad should take Lydia on a trip to see his parents. Brad, would you give us an overview of what you are proposing?" Robert said.

"Robert, can we be a little more relaxed here?" I asked. "I feel like I'm in a board room with a group of trustees or something."

"Sure. I'm sorry," he said. "Brad, how long do you plan to take Lydia away for and where exactly are your parents living now?"

"Okay. My parents are still living in Michigan. I was planning on flying us there. I have tons of frequent flyer miles saved up. It's going to be me and Lydia, as well as Jeannie. Once we get there, my extended family plans on having a reunion of sorts. I was hoping to take her for at least a week. Two, if you guys agree to it."

When he finished Robert gave me a look that seemed to indicate that he didn't have a problem with what Brad was asking for.

"Brad," I said. "That all seems reasonable to me. Two weeks seems maybe a little long, but one week doesn't really seem long enough when you have to travel that far. How do you feel Robert?"

"If you're okay with this, then I am," he said. "All I ask for is that you give us several months' notice, before you want to take her. That way we can make sure that we haven't planned something as well. Maybe we can keep you informed of our plans as we make them, until you get us yours."

"That was easy enough. Almost too easy," Brad said, looking at us with a little puzzlement.

"Well, that may have been easy," I said. "But this next topic sure isn't going to be. I mentioned to both of you that Lydia is starting to ask questions about how Brad is her 'Uncle.' As I've told you, I've put her off about it, but sooner or later she's going to start asking again. And I'd like all of us to have the same answers when we talk to her. I think that it will only confuse her if we each tell her something a little different."

"Agreed," Robert said.

Brad just nodded quietly.

I sat looking at both of them. I wasn't sure how these meetings usually went, but my plan had been to quietly listen at this meeting and I already felt that I had been too vocal. I didn't want them to get suspicious by my showing a lack of knowledge.

Finally Robert spoke, "I guess that we all knew this day was coming. Doesn't make it any easier now that it's here though. My suggestion would be to keep whatever we tell her simple. She still only understands things on a very elementary level. A complicated explanation will only confuse her more."

"I agree with that," Brad said. "Lydia needs a simple explanation, but she's also a bright child. So we need to keep that in mind as we work out what to tell her."

"Brad," I said. "Since this concerns how Lydia interacts with you, why don't you tell us how you feel about this? What would you like us to say?"

Brad gave me a puzzled look, as though he either didn't have an answer or didn't expect to be asked the question. After he thought about it for a moment he replied, "I guess that I'd like her to know that I'm her father. That's what I consider myself to be and that's how I want to be treated by everyone, especially Lydia."

"Okay. And Robert, how do you feel about what we should tell her?" I asked.

"I guess that I'd rather things stay the way that they are, if you want me to be honest. But I'm slowly coming to terms with the fact that they can't. If she's asking questions, then she needs answers. And, as painful as it is for me, I hear what Brad is saying. But I'm used to Lydia thinking that I'm her father. I'm not sure that I want that to change," he said.

Brad nodded, "I understand."

"Okay," I said. "To sum up, we need to keep the explanation simple. Brad, you would like to be acknowledged as being Lydia's father. While Robert, you are trying to come to terms with your role as Lydia's only father changing in her eyes. Is that a fair assessment?"

"Yes," they both said.

"I guess the only thing I'd like to add to this is that I think it's really important that whatever we decide, we tell her the truth," I said. "Because, otherwise, when she gets older and needs a more detailed explanation she will know we lied to her. And that's not a good way for any of us to run our relationship with her. Agreed?"

"Yes," Robert said.

"Absolutely," Brad said. "So the only thing left to figure out is what to say to her."

"Yes," I said, completely throwing my hesitation for speaking to the wind. "As both of you know, I've been wondering lately what we should do. This situation we created is a difficult one. And lately I've been thinking that maybe we did the wrong thing seven years ago when we made our arrangement. Both of you know I've been questioning whether or not we should get a final determination as to who Lydia's biological father is. But both of you gave me very compelling reasons why we shouldn't. And after talking to both of you, I'm also in agreement that we should keep things the way that they are."

I saw both of them were nodding in agreement as I talked. I hoped that they would continue to support me after I finished what I was about to say.

"So I've been thinking," I said. "We came up with a solution seven years ago that works for all of us. Since it's a solution that we all agree that we like, I think that we should be willing to own it in front of Lydia. I'm not suggesting that we tell her how we got into our situation until she gets older and can possibly understand. But what I am suggesting that we tell her that she has two Daddys. And that we don't know who her biological Daddy is. I also think we should start the conversation by telling her that all three of us love her and always will. Maybe we can present it to her by telling her how lucky she is to have more parents than most kids do."

"Someday we are going to have to explain it in detail if we do this now," Robert said. "And her friend's parents are going to ask questions, I'm going to bet."

"But Mary Ann is right," Brad said. "If we all want to live this way then we have to take responsibility for it. And we can tell other adults, who ask, the truth or tell them to mind their own business. The world is pretty crazy these days. This isn't any stranger than some of the other things you hear about, same sex parents or test tube babies."

"Thank you Brad," I said, giving him a smile. "Robert, I know that you feel that you're losing something here, but think about what you do have in comparison. You get to be here everyday when she comes home, you get to read her to sleep every night. You'll always be the Daddy who raised her when she was little. As she grows up all three of us are going to lose certain things that we have with her. Can you just see this as one of those painful steps? Maybe the first step toward the day that she moves off to college or gets place of her own?"

"I suppose so, but let's just take these changes slowly, okay you guys?" he asked. "I don't really like changes that I don't have any control over."

"Then we are in agreement," I said. "Now we only need to decide who is going to be the first one to tell her about this. And I really think that it should be left to Robert to do, if he's willing. Then we can just back up what he says if she wants to talk about it. And I'm betting she'll want to discuss it at some point with each of us."

"I'd be willing to do it if Rob doesn't want to," Brad offered.

"No. I'll do it." Robert said, "But I'm going to need some time to work up to it. Does anyone mind that it's not going to happen instantaneously?"

"I don't mind," I said. "But if Lydia asks me about it again, is it okay if I refer her to you for answers?"

"Yes. And I'll try to do it soon and I'll let both of you know how it goes after I'm done," Robert said.

"Fine," I said. "One more thing that I'd like both of you to think about. No need to answer now. Just something to think about. I'm wondering if, when Lydia gets older and asks more questions, if we shouldn't tell her that she can have a paternity test done once she turns eighteen. I imagine that she wouldn't want to have one by that time, but I think that it's another issue that may come up down the road and I just wanted to put it out there for all of us to mull over."

"Great," Robert said, rolling his eyes. "I can hardly wait for her to grow up now…"

"I'm not sure about that," Brad said. "But I'll think about it too."

"Okay. That sounds good. Meeting officially over?" I asked.

"Yes. Thankfully," Robert said.

"I'm all set," Brad said. "And I've got to get going now. I promised Jeannie I'd get back home in time to go out to dinner. I'll see you two later. Keep me informed. And I'll let you know my vacation plans as soon as I work them out with my parents."

After Brad left, Robert heaved a large sigh, "That was stressful. You okay?"

"Yes. That went better than I thought it would. I was surprised how upset Brad was with me when he came into the room. I wasn't sure that I'd be able to get him to calm down enough to work with us," I said.

"Well, you done good princess," he said as he walked over and put his arms around me. "I'll find someway to do my part and tell her and then hopefully this can all settle down and we can get back to the way things were."

"I know that you'll find the right words to tell Lydia. You're so good at dealing with her. And don't worry. I know she'll always know that you're her Daddy," I said.

"I hope so," he said. "Right now I need to get going to pick her up. Then I'm going to swing by the gallery. I may also run some errands. You're expecting Melissa shortly, right?"

"Yes. I may go downstairs and wait for her. She should be getting here any moment."

"Okay. I'm taking my cell phone in case you need to get a hold of me. I'm out of here," Robert said as he pressed a button on his phone, making sure that it was turned on.

After he left, the house felt calm and quiet. I poured myself the last cup of coffee and then thought about going upstairs to go through more files in Robert's desk, but I was too drained to deal with anymore information. Instead I decided to wait for Melissa downstairs.

When I got to her studio I looked at the paintings that were lying on the floor and leaned against the walls. Not knowing anything about art other than those things that Melissa had explained to me over the years, I had a notion that there were about three different types of styles that she had been exploring. There were the abstract ones with the paint thrown at the canvas; there were ones, like she had painted for me, that were very straightforward in their presentation and, lastly, there were some that seemed to experiment with the illusion of how objects appeared when you looked at them from different angles. When I finished I sat down and watched the world going by outside my house. I wasn't really in the mood to drink more coffee so I just sat my cup on the table in front of me.

I noticed that there was an opened pack of cigarettes under a piece of paper on the table. I decided to smoke one while I waited. Even though I knew intellectually that smoking caused people to become more stimulated, my experience of smoking had always been that it relaxed me. When I finished the cigarette I decided to lie down on the couch. As I waited I found my mind drifting to thoughts about my relationship with Brad in my real life compared to my relationship to Robert in this life. I also felt sad that in this life here, the friendship that the three of us had shared over the years was strained at the very best. Gone were the carefree days of going on mini adventures and taking vacations together. It was sad that the ripple of events that stemmed from one moment on one night so long ago could reach so far. And change things so completely.

CHAPTER 9

▼

I must have fallen asleep because the next thing I knew I was hearing Melissa's voice calling to me.

"Mary Ann. Mary Ann. Come on. It's time to wake up. If you can hear me, then wake up," she said.

I tried to open my eyes, but I must have been very tired because it took a lot of effort to get them open. Once I was able to focus I could see Melissa was sitting next to me, holding my hand. I smiled at her and I saw her face light up with a smile as well.

"Oh good. Lover, you've had all of us quite worried the past couple of days. I'm going to ring the nurse," she said, grabbing some sort of cord that was lying next to me.

It took me a couple of minutes to realize that we weren't in Melissa's studio anymore. We seemed to be someplace where everything was white or stainless steel and given Melissa's comment I was guessing that it was a hospital of some sort.

"Where are we?" I asked.

"Right now you're in San Francisco General Hospital," she said. "But they have been talking about transferring you to somewhere else."

"Why? What happened?"

"Don't you remember? You were walking on a cliff path and you fell and hit your head. Do you remember?"

"Oh yeah. I'm back?"

"Yes. You've been unconscious for several days now. But now you're back."

"I remember falling on the cliff. But how did I get here? And where is Brad?" I asked.

"You have Robert and Crystal to thank for being here. The two of them were in the same cove. When they were walking back, to leave, they saw your scarf blowing in the wind. It was windy and the scarf was so light against the dark wall of the cliff that they noticed it and explored further. When they found you, they called an ambulance. You were brought here right away when Brad heard what happened. He wanted to get you to a good medical facility as fast as possible," she said.

"And my camera?"

"Brad has it." She squeezed my hand, "I'm just so thankful that you woke up. We've all been so worried about you. The doctors seemed confident that you would, but since it was taking so long I was really starting to get worried. And you should see how shook up Brad and Robert are."

"Where is Brad?" I asked again, pretty sure that she hadn't answered me yet.

"Oh yes. He has gone to get your things. You have to be out of the house up there by tomorrow," she said. "Robert is taking a break and getting something to eat. We've been taking turns sitting here with you. Talking to you as much as we can."

"With Crystal?"

"No. Hospitals depress Crystal. Robert took her home the first day that you were in here."

At that point a nurse came into the room. "Well, I see that you decided to wake up," she said. "I'm going to need to take your temperature and then we're going to get some blood drawn. The doctor will be around to see you in a bit as well. I just need for you to rest as much as possible."

"Okay," I said, right before she inserted the thermometer device into my mouth.

It didn't take long for her box to beep that my temperature had registered and for the technician to draw my blood. Then Melissa and I were alone together again.

"Hospitals depress me too," I said in a half-whispered voice.

"Yes. I know. But not in the tragic way that they apparently depress Crystal," she said with some sarcasm.

"Oh... glad to know that I'm not the only one who sees her for who she is," I said.

"It's not just us that are on to her," she said. "I think that Brad has just about had it and Robert didn't seem terribly pleased with her performance either. I

don't know Robert too well, but he didn't look all that happy when he was dealing with her a couple of days ago."

"I just feel so weird," I said. "My head still hurts a little. And I feel so stupid
for being here."

"What do you mean?"

"It's my fault that I'm here. I was following Robert and Crystal. They were
having a fight and I wanted to hear what they were saying, so I followed them.
They took the good path and I took the one that had started to wash out. I was
looking at them through my camera and not paying attention to where I was
standing when I lost my footing and fell. I feel so stupid. Please don't tell anyone."

"Your secret is safe with me," she said. "But it seems that you all were having a
weekend of secrets up there on the coast."

"What do you mean?"

"Brad is beside himself that he left you alone that morning. He went up to
Mendocino to see a Realtor that he's been talking to. That house that you all
were staying in isn't a rental; it's a house for sale. Robert found it and Brad
worked it out so that you could stay there to see if you like it. He's willing to buy
it for you so that you can move back home out here. Closer to where you grew
up. Anyway, he was meeting with the Realtor to see comparables to make sure
that the house was priced right, in case you liked it enough to live there, when
you fell. And he's blaming himself for what happened."

"He's willing to move here?" I asked in disbelief. "I always had the impression
that he didn't want to live in California."

"True, he's not all that hot for it. But he wants you to be happy and he seems
to think he can make it work financially," she said.

"And Robert found the house for us?"

"Yes. He has a good friend who is a Realtor and he's had her searching the
database for something on the coast with a view and some property. I think the
fact that he was involved with finding the house and with helping Brad to keep it
a secret is part of the reason that Crystal is all bent out of shape."

"That explains a lot of things. The fact that the house looked like it had never
been rented before. Crystal's extremely bad behavior. Someday I'll tell you about
her manners at the dinner table the other night. It might also explain why she was
so unhappy to be vacationing there with us. Between you and me, it was like she
was a small pouting child the whole time," I said.

"That might explain why the guys were in such a hurry to get her out of here
then. The minute that she began complaining Robert started walking her out and

took her home. I haven't heard him mention how it went since he returned. But he's been here with Brad and me the whole time. The two of them have been sleeping over at my place," she said. "They are both going to be so relieved to see you awake."

"So you guys have been here the whole time?"

"Yep. Almost all the time there has been one of us here in the room with you. Waiting for you to wake up."

"That's awfully nice of you guys. Really," I said. "But I just had the weirdest experience."

"Really? Tell me about it."

"Where do I start? After I fell on that rocky path, I woke up in a house on top of a hill in San Francisco with a little girl and Robert as my husband. You remember how I always told you that I had a mad crush on him?"

"Yes. I remember. But how did you end up married to him instead of Brad?" she asked.

"That's the interesting part. You remember that night I told you about. The one before the wedding when I had that big fight with Brad and went over to Robert's?"

"Yes. Vaguely."

"It seems that by a strange set of coincidences, I ended up having sex with Robert that night and got pregnant. But only I knew that Lydia, the baby, was Robert's. Everyone else thought that it could be Robert's or Brad's and they had this strange set-up where Lydia basically had two fathers," I said.

"How did you know whose baby it was and did you end up saying anything to them?" she asked.

"I knew because here I never got pregnant and up until the moment that I slept with Robert it seemed that my life was the same as it is here. Since I didn't sleep with Brad after I slept with Robert there, I surmised that the child must have been Robert's. Plus she was the splitting image of him. I just couldn't believe, after looking at her, that anyone would have doubted who her father was," I said.

"But they did?"

"Yes. Everyone did. So I went along with it. But when Lydia looked at me questioningly with those vivid blue eyes, I felt the same way that I do when Robert gives me that look. I was fairly certain that she was Robert's baby even before I learned about when and who I'd had sex with before I had her. It was very odd," I said. "Oh, and you were there as well."

"I was? What was I doing there?"

"You had an art studio on the first floor and a dreamy new boyfriend. Both of us smoked a ton of those clove cigarettes that you used to smoke years ago. Neither of us were health nuts," I said, laughing.

"Oh geeze, I haven't smoked one of those in years. I can't even remember what they taste like," she said, laughing too. "And I sure could use a dreamy new boyfriend. I still have the old, worn-out one hanging around."

"Trust me, you're not missing much on the cigarette front. They were pretty strong and not so good, but for some reason I just couldn't get enough of them. And I had to hide what I was doing from Robert who pretty much wanted to control almost all aspects of my life," I said.

"For some reason, that's not too hard for me to imagine. But, given your age-old crush, how did you like being married to him?"

"That was the really odd part. He was incredibly sweet to me in some ways, but he always seemed to need to be involved with whatever I was doing. Like he told me to make sure to leave you alone so that you could work. And he wasn't too pleased when I put the painting that you gave me for my birthday up in place of something that he had bought and paid a lot of money for," I said. "Although, the next day he did say that he could get used to your painting and then he offered to take back the one that he had bought."

"That was nice of him, I guess," she said. "But tell me more about the painting. What exactly did I paint for you?"

"Oh, it was absolutely beautiful. And if you are ever wondering what I want as a gift, remember I would take this painting. And you'd never have to give me anything else, ever again," I said. "It was a picture of a much younger me standing on the cliffs. Actually, I think that the cliff shot was really was one of the ones that I took outside the house while I was there, now that I think about it. Anyway, I was standing next to a willow tree with these beautiful purple flowers beneath it. They were the color of wisteria. And I was looking out to the ocean. Sort of like I was a sea captain's wife, waiting for his ship to return from a long trip. All the colors in the painting were mostly muted, except for the purple flowers. And there was a slight breeze so my hair and the willow branches were lightly blowing," I said.

"That doesn't sound too difficult. I could probably paint you something like that if you wanted," she said.

"Really? I've always admired your work, but I've been hesitant to ask for anything, given that I know that you are trying to make a living creating art," I said.

"I am, but I could work on it during times that I'm not feeling particularly inspired. It might take me a while, but I could do it, if you want."

"I'd love that. But there's one more thing about it. The feeling of the piece was that of loneliness, but there was also hope, if you know what I mean," I said.

"I think that I have an image of it. I could sketch it and then let you look at it. Before I start using paint, if you want," she said.

"Okay. Thanks. I know that Brad will be thrilled as well."

"Apparently, unlike Robert was."

"Yes," I said, with a chuckle.

Melissa looked at her watch and said, "I'm going to try to call both Robert and Brad on my cell phone, but I have to leave the building to do it. Will you be alright here alone for a few minutes?"

"Sure, I'll be okay. But hurry back, okay?"

"No problem. I just promised to call them both the minute that you woke up so that they could stop worrying," she said as she retrieved her phone from her tote on the floor. "I'll be back in a flash."

After she left I had time to reflect on what had happened. I was feeling pretty lucky that I hadn't fallen all the way down the side of the cliff, because I had been at least a hundred feet above the cove from what I could remember. I was grateful that I must have been able to find solid ground before I hit my head. My hand reached up to where I remembered feeling the pain and felt that there was still some bandaging there. I guessed that I would find out how bad it was when I saw the doctor. But, no matter what, I was feeling pretty good except for the IVs that were stuck in my arm.

Once I had determined that physically I was in pretty good shape my thoughts began to wander to what I had just been through. The other life that I had experienced seemed so real. It was as though it had really happened, not that it was a dream. In dreams things often were disjointed and people didn't necessarily act like themselves. What I had just been through was very different. Everyone had been exactly the way that I remembered; only they behaved differently because they had been through a separate, unique set of events. And those events had changed how they saw the world and reacted to it. I really was puzzled about what had just happened to me. I also wondered how close to reality my alternate life would have been if, in fact, all of us had experienced those pasts.

As I lay there pondering these questions Melissa returned to the room.

"Robert will be here in about ten minutes and Brad should be showing up somewhere between a half hour and an hour after that, depending on traffic. Both of them are anxious to see you and Brad sends his love."

"Yes. I imagine that Brad is racked with guilt."

"Why do you say that?" she asked.

"Well, you already know he was gone the morning that I fell. What you may not know is that the last time we spoke, we had a major fight. After I yelled at him, he walked off down the road to cool off. We disagreed about how I was dealing with the way that Crystal was behaving," I said.

"But you're not really angry with him now, are you?"

"No. I wasn't that angry with him then. I was just hurt and upset by how Crystal had acted at dinner. He was refusing to support my feelings so I was taking it out on him. Thank goodness that he had the sense to leave so that I could calm down," I said.

"I see."

"Yes. But after that I talked to Robert and got some perspective on what was going on. Obviously, even then, I didn't know everything that was happening. But Robert told me enough to make me feel justified about how I felt. And he also told me things that made me feel sympathetic toward her. I was anxious to talk to Brad about what Robert had told me, but we kept missing each other. Then I had the bright idea to follow Robert on his argument with Crystal rather than heading off to take photos like I planned. Big mistake," I said.

"Live and learn. That's what I always say," Melissa said with a smile. "If I were you, I'd just let all of that go. I suspect that the two guys have. Neither of them has mentioned any of this since you got here."

"Probably good advice," I said. "Although, as usual, easier to give than take." I said as I smiled at Melissa. I could feel one of our age-old-sayings games beginning.

"Oh, yeah. Truer words have never been spoken," she said in jest back.

As I was about to throw out another one of our truer-than-true sayings, Robert came into the room.

"So you really are awake. Thank goodness. How are you feeling?" he asked. When he saw that Melissa already occupied the only chair, he sat gently down on the bed next to me.

"Not bad. Considering. I guess," I said.

"I've got to make some calls," Melissa said, excusing herself. "I'll be out in the courtyard if either of you need me."

"I couldn't believe that it was you, lying there, when we climbed that path to see why there was a scarf blowing in the wind. Thank goodness you were wearing it. I'm not sure that we would have found you otherwise. Although, I guess that we would have searched the area sooner or later because your car was parked up by the road," he said.

"Melissa told me how you guys found me. I really thank you and Crystal for coming to see what was attached to that scarf. I still can't believe that I took such a tumble on that path. It looked perfectly fine. Not washed out at all," I said.

"When we got there at least a foot of the path near you was missing. From where we were, we didn't hear or see anything when it went either. I guess that the sound of the waves was louder than the sound of the rocks falling," he said.

"Well, as scary as it was, I guess that all's well that ends well," I said, still in old-sayings-mode, and trying to make light of what happened.

"Ultimately I guess you're right, but you gave us all quite a fright. Especially over the past few days when you wouldn't wake up. Even though you looked so child-like and peaceful sleeping here, it was terrifying that you didn't come to," he said.

"I'm sorry that I scared everyone. But I'm grateful that you all care about me so much."

"You don't need to apologize," he said, giving me a strangely tender look.

Normally, in this situation, I would have been torn between doing one of two things. First, I would have wanted to reach out and put my hand over his, to touch him in some non-sexual, non-threatening way. And then secondly, I would get embarrassed because of what I was thinking about doing and then I would try to change the subject so that he wouldn't be able to look inside my soul and know how it was that I felt about him. As I felt myself drifting through these two emotions, I desperately found myself wanting to change how I acted. But I felt helpless to do anything other than what I was used to.

"So Melissa told me that you and Brad have really been working to find a place for us to buy; not to vacation at," I said. "You both were very good at keeping it a big secret from me. I had no idea what was going on."

"I don't want to steal Brad's thunder, but the plan was for Crystal and I to get lost on the last night and for Brad to tell you that if you wanted, he was willing to buy the house for you," Robert said. "I felt a little odd about keeping it all a secret, but when I thought about it some more, I felt that it was like a little white lie. Like keeping a secret about what he got you for Christmas."

"That's one really big Christmas gift," I said jokingly.

"Yes. I'll say," he said with a smile. "And right now he's feeling like there's no way that you would want to buy that house. Given what happened to you there. He's got a couple more days to let the owners know what you two plan on doing."

"I'm not sure that my being a major klutz would stop me from wanting to live there," I said. "I'm more worried about how we could afford to do it."

"That's not my department madam," he said. "I'm only on the search committee. I do what is requested of me. Glad to know that you liked the house that we located though."

"I really like the location best. And once I learn to follow directions that I read on signs, I probably could manage to live there without killing myself. Otherwise, I'm going to need you to follow around after me, rescuing me from whatever danger I get myself into," I said.

"I could learn to get used to that," he said with a wink.

"That's a sweet thing to say," I said as I heard the muffled sound of a phone ringing.

Robert reached into his pocket and pulled out a cell phone and the ringing sound grew louder. He looked at it and said, "It's Brad. He probably wants a report on how you're doing. Mind if I take it?"

Something inside of me felt an urgency and I heard myself say, "No, don't answer it now."

Robert stopped his finger from hitting the button that would have picked up the call and then he looked at me puzzled for a minute, "Why not? Why don't you want me to take this call?"

As I felt him staring at me, I was reminded of how Lydia looked when she questioned me. I began to worry that he really could see into the deepest reaches of my mind and I began to feel flustered. But I knew the time had come for us to talk, really talk.

"Two reasons really," I said, trying to gather my courage enough to continue. "One is that I don't think that you're supposed to use cell phones in the hospital. There's equipment that the signals can mess with and Melissa said she could only use hers outside. And the other reason is that I think I would like to talk to you more."

"You're right about the phone thing. I forgot," he said, pushing the button that turned the phone off. Once he did that the ringing stopped, "So what exactly is it that you want to talk about?"

Again I was sensing the easiest thing to do would be to just run away from my feelings. To tell him something that wasn't that important and then to act like that was what I'd made a big deal out of. But, instead, I got together as much determination as I could muster and started.

"This isn't easy, but I need to tell you some things. Things about the past. Things that I think about when I'm around you," I said. "And I'm not sure why I feel that I need to do it now, but I do. Well, maybe it's because of what I just went through. Having a bad accident and all. Maybe I'm realizing that neither you nor I are going to live forever. And maybe I'm feeling that I'd like you to know what I want to say just in case something bad does happen to one of us."

"This sounds pretty serious," he said.

"Oh no. Then I'm probably not doing this right," I said. "I don't mean to make a big deal out of telling you this. I really don't want what I'm about to tell you to change anything at all. I just want you to know what I'm thinking and feeling. Or what I've been thinking and feeling all these years that I've known you."

"Okay. Got it. Just information," he said, waiting for me to continue.

I was finding that the more that I talked, the easier it got to do. However, so far it felt like all I had managed to do was to babble incoherently. So I took a deep breath to steady myself and continued.

"Before I ever met you, I saw you. You didn't see me, but it was during that first week of college. I was eating my lunch, sitting on the main quad, and I saw you walk by. I found that I couldn't take my eyes off of you. After you had passed by I got up and tried to follow you. You went into the Chemistry building and I thought that you had gone into one of the lecture rooms. But I couldn't find you by the time that the class began to start, so I left," I said.

Robert sat across from me, and I felt he was patiently waiting for me to get to the point of my story.

"After that I met Brad and we began to get to know one another as friends and then things got more serious," I continued. "I was quite surprised the day I walked into his kitchen and found you sitting there. Pleasantly surprised. And over the years I've enjoyed getting to know you better. But in some ways it's been really hard."

"I'm not sure exactly what it is you're trying to tell me."

"Yes. I know. Even while I'm telling you, I'm having a hard time saying what it is that I want to say," I said. I was finding this more difficult than I had feared.

"I guess what I'm really trying to tell you is that ever since that first moment when I saw you, I've felt as though I'm in love with you. And until now I haven't really understood why I didn't do something about it. Why I didn't tell you about it," I said.

By this time I was looking down at the ground, unable to raise my eyes to see how Robert was reacting to what I was saying.

"Go on," he said quietly.

"Okay. I guess what I've been the most puzzled about over the years is why I never said anything. If you'd asked me a week ago, I'd have told you that the reason was that I didn't want to hurt Brad. Because as you know, I really do love

Brad. Or I'd have told you I felt that you were too honorable of a person and that I felt I'd have diminished how you saw me if you knew I was 'emotionally cheating' on my husband by having feelings for you. I had a neat little list of reasons that always kept me from telling you how I felt," I said. "But now I think that the reason I didn't tell you how I felt was because I was afraid of you in a way."

"Afraid of me? What did I ever do to make you afraid of me?"

"Oh, I'm not afraid you would do something to hurt me. It's more that I'm afraid that because of how much I was in love with you, that I would have let you control me. That I would have lost who I am. My independence. My personality," I said. "I was afraid that because of who I am I would have spent my time trying to please you, rather than trying to find the things that make me happy with myself. My fear doesn't come from something you would have done to me. It's what I would have done to myself in response to how I felt about you. And I don't think you would have had a whole lot of control over how I reacted to you."

"I see," he said. "Just to satisfy my curiosity. How does that differ with how you are with Brad, if you don't mind saying."

"Well, with Brad I don't have that overwhelming feeling of needing to please him in order to keep him loving me. I feel we are friends more than lovers, although we are lovers in every sense of the word," I said, again feeling that I was beginning to babble. "I guess the difference is that being with Brad adds to my existence; whereas, if I was with you I'd be on an emotional roller coaster, worried about whether I was making you happy or not. Unable to breathe if I felt you were upset with me."

Having finished the hard part of what I wanted to say I mustered the courage to look up at Robert. I found that he was looking down at the ground as though he was deep in thought. We sat in silence until he finally spoke.

"So, what you're saying is, if you had loved me less and met me first, you would have been interested in pursuing a relationship with me?"

"Yes. I guess so. But honestly, if I'd met you first I'd probably have gone for the relationship, regardless of how I felt. It's only in retrospect that I can see why I stayed with Brad. He's emotionally rock solid and that's something I've come to appreciate. And I wouldn't have known how that felt if I hadn't gone out with him," I said.

"Wow. I guess that timing *is* everything after all," he said, shaking his head in disbelief.

"What do you mean?" I asked.

"Before I met Brad I had seen the two of you waiting in line to go see a movie on a pleasant spring evening. I remember distinctly noticing you first. You were laughing at something and you seemed so natural, so assured of yourself. I remembered thinking that whatever bastard you were with must be very lucky. And then I noted your partner, Brad. When I saw him in one of my classes later that year, I struck up a conversation with him. I was as fascinated with who he was, as I was with you. I wanted to know what kind of guy a woman like you would pick. But the more I got to know him the more I began to respect him. By the time I met you I felt that you were as lucky to have him, as he was to have you," he said.

I sat and listened in surprised silence. I almost said something when he paused, but then thought better of it, wanting to allow him to continue if he had more to say.

"And it's possible there's something to what you say about my tendency to want to change things," he said as he got up and looked out of the window. "One of the things I respect most in Brad is that he's content to sit by and watch you as you live your life. This may sound silly, but it's as though you were a butterfly that he enjoys watching fly around. And occasionally, when you land on his hand he's content to stay still and watch you until you fly away again. I'm afraid that I would be tempted to touch your wings which would make the dust, that allows you to fly, come off. If we were together I'd have to check and double-check all the time to make sure I wasn't doing that. This way actually is easier. I can sit back and watch you just the way that Brad does because I don't have any romantic involvement in how you behave."

I lay still in the bed, watching him look at what was going on outside, unable to see whatever he was looking at. I was feeling very close to him, even though physically we were quite a distance apart.

"I think I'm quickly becoming a professional bachelor at this point too," he continued. "As the years go by, and as I date more women, I've come to the conclusion that I like things the way that I like them and I doubt I'm going to find someone who is going to fit the ideal I have in my mind as a wife. I'm slowly coming to terms with the idea that I'm meant to be single."

"I'm not sure that's what fate has in store for you," I said. "But, if you don't mind my saying this, I think that you need to find a different type of woman if you're really looking for a wife."

"I don't mind you talking about this. What do you mean?" he asked.

"Let me first say that I'm certainly no expert at this. And, I guess, I need to point out that you should probably take what I say with a grain of salt because it's possible I'm speaking out of jealously. But I think I can say with a fair deal of moral certainty that a person who acts only in their best self-interest, the way that Crystal does, isn't the ideal mate for you," I said.

"What exactly are you talking about?"

"Okay. Let's take her behavior at dinner the other night, as an example. If she really cared for you she would put your interests first. Like we did, for example, when she made us that liver stew. We cared enough for you to eat the stew and tell her we liked it. On the other hand, she didn't care enough for you to even manage to be polite to me when I cooked dinner for us. Now, Melissa told me that there were other things going on as well with her. Like her being upset that you helped look for the house and all. But, really, how hard would it have been to eat some of the food. And how hard would it have been to move the ribs neatly from one plate to the other instead of throwing them. You need someone who spends some time making sure your needs are met, instead of only worrying about their own needs," I said. "And if you end up marrying someone like that I can only imagine their behavior would become amplified over the passage of time. I don't believe you can change a person when you marry them. If anything, they become more set in their ways because they are no longer trying to be on their best behavior in order to get you to be romantic with them."

Robert turned around as I talked. "I think you are right about that. And, just so you don't worry, I think things with Crystal are almost over."

"Thank goodness," I said. "I've been afraid to say anything about this to you. But sitting here thinking about it, I realized it would be a lot worse if we had to talk about this ten years from now, after you married her and lived with her and possibly had children with her. She's a very beautiful woman, but I don't think she's a very happy one. And it's not clear to me that anyone will ever be able to make her happy enough so that she worries about other people's feelings, especially yours."

"I've been slowly realizing that. And I don't mind you telling me what you think of my romantic interests. I've always been a little puzzled about why you and Brad haven't said anything about any of them over these past years," he said.

"Well, just for the record. I really liked the one who wore cowboy boots and went western dancing. I can't think of her name, but I remember her fondly," I said.

"Oh yes. That was Nancy. She ended up leaving me because she decided to go back to her husband. I liked her a lot too. She was a free spirit," he said.

"Yes, Nancy was it. She had a wonderful laugh too. Too bad that she worked things out with her ex. You two got along well. Although she might have been just a little bit too much of a free spirit. But that would have shaken up your world in kind of a good way, I think."

"Yes. That's what I need," he said, walking toward me. He then sat down again on the bed beside me and said in a slightly mocking manner. "I need my world shaken up."

"Don't look at me," I said jokingly back. "After what I've just been through, I need security. Feet planted firmly on the ground and all."

Inside I felt happy. I could tell that things were back to the way they were before we had our talk. I had been able to tell him what I needed, and he had heard what I wanted him to hear. Later, when I was alone, I'd take some time and think about the new things I had learned from him. But for now I was secure in our friendship and I felt a new sense of freedom from having finally told him my long held secret.

"Why, someone sounds like they are feeling much better," I heard Brad say as he walked in.

"I would like to think it comes from my magical healing powers," Robert said jokingly. "But, in truth, I think she is just about the same as I found her. I'll let you two be alone." As he got up to leave the room he looked at me and said, "We'll finish our talk some time later in the future."

I smiled at Robert in agreement and then turned my attention to Brad. "Hey. Long time, no see, stranger."

"I'll say. I've been so worried about you," he said.

"I'm okay. At least I think so. The doctor is supposed to show up at some point. But I'm figuring that I'm okay or they would have rushed someone in to see me by now."

"The doctor told me that he thought you would have a full recovery. And the true miracle is that you didn't fall over the side of that cliff," he said. "I'm so grateful to Robert and Crystal for finding you. And I'm sorry I wasn't there myself that morning."

"Don't feel bad. It's more my fault than yours that I was there that morning. I really should have followed directions and stayed off that path. I just thought I could tell if it was okay or not. Obviously I couldn't," I said. "But Melissa told me you were off talking to a Realtor about us possibly buying the house. Is that true?"

"Yes. Actually, it's true. But I'm guessing you aren't going to want to live someplace where you had such an unpleasant experience. I asked the Realtor if we could have more time before we have to make up our minds, but I also told her I didn't think that you'd be interested after what happened to you," he said as he sat down on the bed next to me and reached over to hold my hand.

"I don't hate the house because I foolishly tried to walk on the wrong trail," I said. "But I'd have to think about whether or not we should buy it. Not the least of my concerns is exactly how you propose that we afford it and earn a living out here."

Brad looked at me and smiled. "Well, I have some good news to tell you."

"What?"

"I've been working on something sort of in secret. I didn't want to tell you because I didn't want to spoil the surprise or disappoint you if it didn't work out," he said. "Do you remember that large account that I've been working on for the past two years? The one that always seemed like it was close to working out, but then I never could get George to actually sign on the dotted line?"

"Yes. Who could forget?"

"Well, the day before we left for vacation I met with him and he signed a ten-year contract. I insisted he agree to a ten-year time frame because I was afraid that he'd put me through the same torture when it came time to renew. Anyway, we are now a national company with enough money coming in to live anywhere we want."

"I didn't even know that you were working on something with him now," I said. "I just figured he'd always be the 'big deal that never happened.' I'm so proud of you."

"Why thanks," he said. "I've got to say that I had just about given up on him as well. But when I stopped calling him all the time, he suddenly started calling me and finally things worked out. Now, I don't want you to worry about it, but just think about whether or not you want the house. I'm willing to move out here and live anywhere you want, but you've always talked about how much you love the coast and I really like the location."

"I love the location too, but that house isn't exactly my dream house. It's nice, but not exactly what I've dreamed of," I said.

"I understand that and I agree with you. But I've been thinking maybe we should buy it and renovate it or add to it until it is our dream house. It will take time, but we have all the time in the world," he said.

"Interesting idea. I will think about it. How long do we have to decide?"

"The Realtor has asked the owner to extend our deadline, given what happened. I gave them a deposit so we have more time. Don't worry. Just think about it," he said.

"Okay. I will," I said. "By the way, I'm sorry we fought about Crystal. I wanted to say I was sorry and to tell you something I found out, but we just never crossed paths. I don't want you to think I'm still upset about it."

"Don't worry about it," he said. "I talked to Rob about Crystal and it seems that you were more right than me this time. I was just trying to be fair to her. Something I quickly got over when she started acting out here at the hospital. I don't think Rob is going to date her much longer. At least I hope not."

"After you left that night, Robert told me she is weird about what she eats, because of her modeling jobs, and that she had been nasty to someone else who cooked for her. And then the next morning they got into a fight and she made it pretty clear she really doesn't like me. And, I don't think that I like her," I said.

"You don't have to like her. You only need to be civil to her if Rob continues to date her. I won't criticize you about your feelings toward her ever again," he said.

"Thank you. I don't think that you'll ever know what that means to me," I said.

"I have some idea," he said as he squeezed my hand. "By the way, you said the doctor hadn't come to see you yet?"

"Yes. That's right."

"Well, I think I'm going to go find him and make sure he sees you soon," he said as he got up and started to leave the room.

When he reached the door I said, "Brad?"

"Yes?" he said as he turned around to look at me from the doorway.

"I've been thinking about our sex life, and I think there are a few things I'd like to talk to you about trying, if you're interested."

"You got it," he said, with a big smile.

978-0-595-36047-5
0-595-36047-5

Printed in the United States
37414LVS00005B/217-225

9 780595 360475